If You Had a Horse

"Sire," said the merchant, "I beg you to look at this horse. All the marvels you have today are as nothing compared with him."

All the horses in this rich and colourful collection are sumptious, dashing and marvellous! From the flying horse of a Persian prince to a bucking Palomino of the Wild West. From the nag that lead Finn MacCool and his fellow Celts, to the Greek Gods' horses of the Sun.

Feast your mind on this marvellous collection of tales drawn from the world's rich heritage of myth, legend and folklore.

Nine stories engagingly retold by Margaret Hodges.

If You Had a Horse

Margaret Hodges

Illustrated by D Benjamin van Steenburgh

Hippo Books
Scholastic Publications Limited
London

Scholastic Publications Ltd.,
10 Earlham Street, London WC2H 9RX, U.K.

Scholastic Inc.,
730 Broadway, New York, NY 10003, U.S.A.

Scholastic Tab Publications Ltd.,
123 Newkirk Road, Richmond Hill,
Ontario, L4C 3G5, Canada

Ashton Scholastic Pty. Ltd.,
P O Box 579, Gosford, New South Wales,
Australia

Ashton Scholastic Ltd.,
165 Marua Road, Panmure, Auckland 6,
New Zealand

First published simultaneously in Canada and the United States of
America by Charles Scribner's Sons, 1984.

First published in the United Kingdom by Scholastic Publications
Limited, 1987
Text copyright © Margaret Hodges, 1984
Illustrations copyright © D Benjamin van Steenburgh, 1984.

Quotation on page 33 from Kuno Meyer's translation of "The Isles of
the Happy" from *Selections from Ancient Irish Poetry*, published by
Constable Publishers, United Kingdom. Reprinted by permission from
the publisher.

ISBN 0 590 70568 7

All rights reserved

Phototypeset in Plantin by
AKM Associates (UK) Ltd
Ajmal House, Hayes Road, Southall, London
Made and printed in the Netherlands
by Drukkerij Giethoorn, Meppel

For Helen and Charles Moore

This cavalcade "came west with men who rode from the land where horses were tamed, which is unknown".

(J F Campbell's note in his manuscript collection now deposited in the Advocates' Library, Edinburgh)

"How the horse dominated the mind of the early races . . . . You were a lord if you had a horse. Far back, far back in our dark soul the horse prances . . . . The horse, the horse!"

D H Lawrence: *Apocalypse*

Contents

The Ebony Horse

In the days when Schahriar was sultan from Persia to the borders of China, the storyteller Scheherazade won undying fame for the tales she told every night to the sultan. At the end of one thousand and one nights he married her so that she could go on telling him stories forever. "The Ebony Horse" is one of the tales of those "Abrabian Nights".

THERE WAS ONCE a mighty sultan of Persia who was blessed with two children: a noble son, heir to the throne, and a daughter as fair as the shining moon. The sultan celebrated every New Year's Day with a great feast in his capital city of Shiraz, seated in his courtyard with the young prince and princess beside him, while musicians filled the air with sweet music and inventors from every part of his kingdom showed him strange and curious things that they had made. Whatever was new and marvellous he bought to

add to his treasure-house.

One year the sultan had bought many treasures. When the feast was nearly ended and while he still sat with his children beside him, a foreign merchant, very old and ugly, entered the courtyard, pulling a beautiful horse by the reins. Its body was made of ebony, its mane and tail of ivory. The saddle, too, was ivory, studded with jewels. And the horse was made with such artistry that he seemed alive.

"Sire," said the merchant, "I beg you to look at this horse. All the marvels you have bought today are as nothing compared with him."

"He appears to be finely made," said the sultan, "but my artists could make one as fine."

"You speak only of his appearance," said the merchant. "What the eye does not see is even finer. Inside this horse are devices by which he can carry his rider anywhere in the world with the speed of the wind. That is to say, he flies."

"If this is true, prove it," answered the sultan. "At the foot of yonder mountain grows a palm tree. Fly there and bring me back a leaf from that tree."

The merchant mounted and touched a spot on the horse's shoulder near the saddle. Then to the amazement of all, horse and rider rose into the air and flew swiftly towards the mountain of the palm tree. In a few minutes they returned, and the ebony horse came smoothly to earth before the sultan's throne. In the hand of the merchant was a palm leaf, which he presented with a low bow.

The sultan was obsessed with desire to own the wonderful horse. "Name your price," he said to the merchant.

"The price is high," replied the man. "You must know that I did not make this horse. It was given to me by the inventor in exchange for my daughter. She made me promise to give up the horse only in exchange for a gift as precious as herself. Therefore, give me your daughter and I will give you the ebony horse."

The whole court laughed at the insolence of this offer, but the sultan wanted the horse so much that he sat silent and doubtful. Then the young prince leaped to his feet saying, "My father, have nothing to do with this trickster".

"Perhaps you are right, my son," answered the sultan. "At least let us try the horse for ourselves before I make a bargain."

At this, the prince mounted the horse, and the merchant, seeing success almost in his hands, willingly showed the spot where a touch of hand would make the horse rise into the air. Instantly the prince and the horse took flight, drifting with the wind.

"Wait! Wait!" shouted the merchant. "I have not told you how to come back!"

It was too late. The prince and the ebony horse were gone.

"He may fall into the sea!" the sultan cried with a groan. Then he ordered his guards to throw the merchant into prison, saying, "If the prince does not return, you shall die!"

As for the prince, he was now so high above the earth that the mountains of Persia appeared as flat as the plains, and often he saw nothing but a white sea of cloud beneath him. It was certainly time to descend. He examined the neck and back of the horse and pressed here and there, but to no avail. The horse only continued to rise on the currents of air. Then the prince noticed a small handle, shaped like the head of a cock and hidden behind the horse's right ear. He turned this and the horse shot rapidly up, even higher.

"There must be another handle," the prince reasoned. And so there was, hidden behind the horse's left ear. This the prince turned and at once began to descend towards the earth. Now that he could control the horse, he began to enjoy his flight.

As night came on the prince found himself flying over a strange country and saw below him a city with palaces and gardens. He thought that he had better spend the night in this city and guided the horse downwards until it came to rest on the flat roof of a palace. There he dismounted and began to feel his way about in the dark, hoping to find someone who might help him.

He made his way carefully down a flight of steps into a marble courtyard and on into one splendid room after another, all of them full of sleeping guards and servants. At last he saw a light shining from behind a curtained doorway and, entering there, beheld the most beautiful princess in the world. She lay asleep on a sofa piled with silken cushions and surrounded by her serving women, who slept on low couches around her.

The prince knelt beside her and lightly touched her arms. At this, she opened her eyes, and seeing that he looked gentle as well as handsome, she did not cry out but listened while he spoke softly to her.

"Madam, I am a prince of Persia. I am here in a strange land without friends and perhaps in danger. I appeal to you for help."

The princess answered, "I, too, am of royal birth. This is the land of Yemen and the king, my father, has given me this palace for my pleasure. My serving women will bring you food and fresh linen. Tomorrow morning when you have rested, come to me again and tell me by what adventure you came here so far from Persia."

The prince was given a perfumed bath and a soft bed, where he slept soundly until morning.

When he awoke he found the princess waiting for him, dressed in the finest silks, her head crowned with diamonds, her neck and arms circled with flashing emeralds, and her eyes sparkling brighter than any of these.

"Now," she said, "tell me how you came here."

When the prince's story was told, he took her hand and said, "Princess, I must return to my father, who surely thinks me dead. And yet I am your prisoner here unless you will consent to return with me to Persia and be my wife. I am determined never to be separated from your loveliness so long as I live."

At first the princess begged him to stay with her in Yemen. She made him sit beside her in a little room hung with blue and gold. Servants brought sweet fruits and filled the air with the sound of lutes and zithers. But the prince said, "Princess, I will give you a palace even lovelier in Persia. Do not tempt me to stay."

Then she begged him at least to ask the consent of her father for the marriage. But the prince said, "If your father does not consent, he may have me killed, alone and unarmed as I am. I ask only the consent of your own heart."

At last the princess put her hand in his and he led her to the roof of the palace. He mounted the ebony horse, drew the princess up behind him, and they rose into the air.

The horse flew so swiftly and the prince guided him so well that a few hours brought them to Persia and the city of Shiraz. The prince thought it best to leave the princess in a summer palace outside of the city while he himself went to explain matters to the sultan and to prepare a proper welcome for a royal bride. He left the ebony horse with her and ordered one of the horses from the stables to be saddled for his ride into the city.

The people of Shiraz, who had thought him dead, made the streets echo with shouts of joy when he came riding in and passed through the palace gate. The sultan clasped his son to his heart and, when he heard how things stood, quickly consented to his marriage with the princess of Yemen. He ordered the foreign merchant to be released from prison and told him to be gone forever with his ebony horse.

The wily merchant went at once to the sultan's summer palace outside the city. There he found not only the ebony horse but the princess of Yemen as well. He bowed low to her and said that he had come from the prince with orders to bring her and the ebony horse to the sultan's palace in Shiraz.

The princess, suspecting no harm, mounted the horse behind the merchant, who was soon flying with her into the air. Maliciously he guided the horse over the city so that all could see his triumph and his revenge. The sultan and the prince, who were about to set off to meet the princess at the summer palace, instead saw her carried away into the clouds above them, where she vanished from sight.

The prince was wild with grief, but rather than give way to despair, he vowed to find the princess if he had to travel to the ends of the earth. He disguised himself as a wandering holy man and went from city to city and into far lands asking for news of the wonderful horse and the beautiful princess of Yemen. As he travelled, his beard grew long and his clothing became ragged, so that no one could have guessed him to be a noble young prince.

At last he came to a certain city in Cashmere where he heard some merchants talking in a bazaar. One of them said, "Let me tell you about an adventure that I heard of on my travels. The king of this country was hunting one day and came to an oasis in the desert. There he saw a fine horse made of ebony. The owner of the horse was old and ugly, but he had with him a lady as fair as the sun shining in the blue sky. Since she seemed to be in some distress, the king questioned the man, who pretended that the beautiful lady was his wife. But she cried out, 'He is a liar and an imposter. I am not his wife. I am a princess of Yemen, and he has stolen me away from the noble prince of

Persia whom I was to marry.' Then the king threw the lying villain into prison and took the princess to his own palace. What became of the ebony horse I do not know. The king is determined to marry the princess, but it is said that she has gone mad. The king has offered to give a great reward to any doctor who can cure her, and every doctor of the royal court has tried to heal her. But as soon as they come near her, she falls to the floor and beats her breast and tears her hair, so that she is worse than before.''

When the prince heard these words, he procured a doctor's long robe and went with all speed to the palace of Cashmere, where he presented himself to the king, saying, "I am a physician of Persia, where, as you know, sire, doctors are skilled in the art of healing. I have come to cure the princess. Will you tell me the circumstances which led to her illness?''

The king repeated the story that had already been told in the bazaar. When he had finished, the prince asked, "Where is the ebony horse? I believe that it may be the means of healing the princess.''

"The horse is in my treasure-house,'' the king replied.

"I beg to see it,'' said the prince. And when he was led to the king's treasure-house, he found the horse, perfect in every respect so far as he could see.

"Now take me to the princess,'' said he, and this also was done.

When the princess saw the king entering her chamber with the supposed doctor, she cried out and fell to the floor, tearing her hair and beating her breast. But in truth she was only pretending madness in order to keep all physicians at a distance and so delay her marriage to the king.

Asking the king not to come near, the prince went to the princess and whispered into her ear, "Madam, I am a prince of Persia."

Hearing these words, spoken in the voice she had longed to hear, the princess was faint with surprise and joy. Then to his amazement the king saw that she became calm and listened attentively as the bearded doctor continued to whisper, "Have courage, my beloved! I have come to rescue you. Do exactly as I say and all will be well. When the king comes to visit you tomorrow, receive him in good spirits and consent to the marriage. Never fear, you shall marry no one but myself."

The prince then led the king from the chamber and said to him privately, "The princess is already well on her way to recovery. Through my arts I see that she has been possessed by an evil genie, which entered in some way because of her flight on the ebony horse. Therefore, have the horse brought into your courtyard tomorrow. Let the princess be dressed for her wedding and mounted on the horse. Before your very eyes I shall then complete the cure and restore the princess to perfect health. She will soon be a happy bride."

The king offered the pretended doctor a large bag of gold for his services, but the prince refused with a low bow, saying, "Tomorrow I will claim my reward."

The next day the ebony horse was brought

from the king's treasury into the courtyard. Word had spread through the city about the miraculous cure that was about to take place, and an immense crowd gathered. The prince declared that all, even the king, must stand back at a distance. Then he led the princess from the palace, and she was as lovely as the sun and the moon and all the stars in the heavens. She was clothed in rainbow silks and her jewels were worth a king's ransom.

Gently the prince lifted her into the ivory saddle. He put the reins in her hands. Around the horse he set braziers full of burning coals and threw into them powders that blazed up red and green and blue, giving off a sweet odour.

"Now, sire," he said to the king, "I shall repeat certain magic words that will drive out the evil genie. As the final step in the cure of the princess I shall mount the ebony horse myself, and all her troubles will be ended."

The prince walked three times around the horse, muttering strange words. Thick smoke now rose from the burning braziers. Suddenly the king saw rising from the smoke the ebony horse with the princess and the prince seated upon his back.

The prince called down, "Learn from this that he who wishes to marry a princess should first win her heart."

Then the king saw the prince turn a little handle behind the horse's right ear, and a moment later horse and riders were only a speck in the sky.

This time the prince took no chances but rode the ebony horse straight to his father's palace in

Shiraz; where soon afterwards he married the princess. The brilliant ceremony was delayed only until the blessing of her father, the king of Yemen, could be obtained. This was not long in coming, for he knew that the prince would some day rule over Persia, and to sit at the side of the sultan of Persia was a fate worthy even of a princess of Yemen.

Horses of the Sun

IN THE DAYS when the world was young, the greatest of all the Greek gods was Zeus, who hurled the thunderbolts. The goddess of the earth, the god of the sea, the spirits of every hill and stream acknowledged Zeus as their king. But Apollo too was very powerful—Apollo, the god of the sun, who drove his fiery chariot from dawn to dusk through the blue sky arching over green earth and wine-dark sea.

Sometimes the gods married humans and had children who were half human, half god. One of these was a boy named Phaeton.

Phaeton was a boaster, and he had much to boast about, for he was strong of arm and swift of foot, the winner of every game and contest in his village. But one thing troubled him. There was only a mother at home, and no father. Phaeton did not know who his father was. His mother always turned away from the question.

Among the village boys there was a saying,

"If you do not know who your father is, he must be a nobody." This saying gnawed at Phaeton. Each day he set himself to prove his strength, his courage, and his cleverness. In this way he would prove that he was the son of a father superior to all others in the village.

One morning he raced to the river with the other boys, and ran so fast that he was soon far ahead. Then, just before he reached the river, he stumbled and fell. Everyone laughed at him.

Phaeton jumped up, shouting, "I will beat you next time."

"You will never beat me," said one boy. "I am the son of Zeus."

"My father, too, is powerful," cried Phaeton. "I am sure of it!" But the other boys went off, jeering. Phaeton ran home to find his mother.

"Tell me who my father is," he demanded. "I have begged you many times to tell me. Now I must know. I can no longer bear to be treated like a child at home and like a fool by the whole village."

Phaeton's mother put her hand on his shoulder. "They need not laugh at you," she said. "Your father is very great. He is greater than any man."

"He is a god?" asked Phaeton. This was even more than he had hoped. His eyes shone with excitement.

"Your father is a god almost as powerful as Zeus himself," she answered. "He is . . . Phoebus Apollo! That is why you are named Phaeton, the shining one."

"My father is the sun god!" cried Phaeton.

Full of triumph, he ran off to tell the village boys.

But they would not believe him. "That is a likely story," they taunted. "Do you expect anyone to believe such a tale?"

Phaeton defied them. "It is true! I can prove it so that everyone will know. I will go to see my father in his palace. I will return to tell you about wonders there that no man has ever seen. I will see them with my own eyes."

"Of course," they answered. "You would go away for a day or two and come back with some story that you had invented."

Phaeton was furious. "I *will* prove that I am the son of Apollo," he shouted. "I will ask my father to let me drive his chariot for a day, and you will see me do it!"

Before they could reply, he set off on his long journey. All day and all night he travelled east to the end of the earth and far, far beyond. At last he came to the great golden gates of the sun god's palace. It was dawn. The gates swung open, and light poured out, so bright, so blinding, that Phaeton covered his eyes with his hands.

"Father!" he cried. "Phoebus Apollo!"

Then he heard a voice coming out of the brightness. "So you have come at last. It is a long way, my son. I will take off my crown of rays, and you and I will talk face to face."

Phaeton raised his eyes and beheld the sun in all his glory. Apollo was robed in purple. The Season, the Year, the Month, the Day, and the Hour stood around a glittering throne where the god, his face shining in wisdom and majesty, looked kindly at Phaeton.

The boy was silent, dazzled by the splendour of the palace and by the knowledge that now, at long last, he saw his father. Then, remembering his mission, he stepped to the very foot of Apollo's throne and asked impetuously, "Father, light of the world, I know that you can do anything."

"Anything you like," said Apollo, smiling.

"Would you promise to do something for me?"

"Because you are my son," said Apollo, "I will make a sacred promise, the promise that not even a god can break. I swear by the river Styx that flows between the land of the living and the land of the dead."

"Then," said Phaeton, "let me drive your chariot for a day."

Apollo's bright face clouded. At last he shook his head. "None but myself can drive the chariot. Not even Zeus, whose terrible right arm hurls the thunderbolt."

"Father, you promised," said Phaeton.

Apollo frowned. "The horses are wild. The road is dangerous! The first part is steep. Though the horses are fresh, they can hardly climb it. At noon the path is high up in the starry heavens. Even I feel faint when I look down from that dizzy height on all the earth and sea below. And my horses must follow a straight path while the heavens turn round and round, carrying the constellations with them."

Again the boy urged. Again the father warned. "I must avoid the slashing horns of Taurus, the huge Bull, the bow and arrows of

17

Sagittarius, the Archer. The Lion threatens the horses if they pass too close. The Scorpion and the Crab reach out their sharp claws. The Great Bear roars and growls."

Phaeton hardly listened.

His father continued. "Could you drive a safe course through all these dangers? And at the end of the day the way slopes steeply down to Ocean's caves. If I did not hold the horses back with all my strength, I would fall headlong. What would become of you?"

The heedless youth only answered, "You promised by the river Styx."

That was, after all, a promise that Apollo could not break. Much against his will he ordered the high chariot to be prepared. He told Phaeton to hold the reins tightly. "The path is well worn," he said. "It is the middle path, neither too high nor too low. Keep to it."

He made Phaeton rub a soothing ointment on his skin to protect him from the fierce rays of the sun crown. The white horses were led out from the stable, snorting and stamping, breathing fire.

"I will tell you the names of my horses," said Apollo. "If they become too wild, speak to them by name. The first is Pyrois, whose name means fiery heat. Next is Eous, whose fire lights the sky of dawn. The third is Aethon, heavenly fire. Last comes Phlegon, raging fire. The glow of his breath reddens the western sky at the end of day. Phlegon is the wildest of all my horses."

The golden chariot with its silver wheels stood gleaming at the gates. Impatient to be gone, Phaeton stepped in and took the reins in his hands. His father put the great crown of rays on the boy's head. At once, they were off.

The horses rushed up into the air, carrying Phaeton into the clouds. White mist whirled around him. All he could hear was the wild pounding of hoofs. Then suddenly they were above the morning clouds, and Phaeton saw the road before him, climbing up, high into the blue heavens.

At last! he thought. Now everyone will know who I am. They will never dare to laugh at me again! But the horses felt the difference between the great weight of the god and the light body of the boy. They knew that the hands on the reins were young and untried. Faster and faster beat the great hoofs. Phaeton began to be afraid.

"The horses!" he cried. "They are stronger than I thought! The reins are cutting my hands. Back! Back on the road! Ah! . . . the horses will not obey me! What are their names? I have forgotten the names! I have lost the road!" His voice died away in the empty sky.

Down on earth men saw a strange sight. The sun zigzagged to the north, then to the south. Next it shot so high into the heavens that day turned to night. The chariot of the sun now seemed like a distant start. Phaeton was among the constellations. With terror he remembered his father's words as he saw shapes moving around him.

The chariot rushed towards the Great Bear. Phaeton heard it growl and roar. The horses raced on straight toward the Lion with its terrible jaws and sharp teeth. And now Phaeton heard an angry hiss as cruel claws tore at the legs of the galloping horses.

"The Scorpion!" he cried. "Father! Father! Save me!"

It was too late. The terrified horses leaped from the Scorpion and downward. Out of the heavens plunged the sun, down towards the earth, nearer and nearer. The people saw it reeling towards them. The heat was so intense that fountains and streams dried up. Where green valleys had been, deserts appeared. The sea boiled. Whole cities burned. Phaeton saw it all. He heard the goddess of the earth and the god of the sea praying to Zeus for help.

At that moment the horses turned and began to climb. Phaeton dropped the reins and clung to the chariot. The horses, unrestrained, rushed away into the farthest reaches of the sky, where there was no path. To men's eyes the sun became smaller and smaller until it disappeared. Again the world grew dark, and at last, cold.

"Everything will die!" cried the people. "Zeus! Save us! Stop the sun!"

From the heavens came a great roll of thunder and a mighty crash. Zeus had heard the prayer of the people. He had thrown his thunderbolt at the charioteer, and Phaeton fell from the sky. With his hair on fire, like a shooting star he fell, down, down, through endless oceans of air. The horses galloped down the slope of the western sky, returning to Apollo with the empty chariot.

The river near Phaeton's village home received his body and cooled it forever. They buried his body by that river, and those who buried him said that his face wore the smile that lights the faces of the gods in sorrow as in joy, in defeat as in triumph. His spirit passed over that other stream, the river Styx, which divides the living from the dead. On the far side, the spirit of Phaeton lived on forever.

Phaeton's friends lived to be old men in the village and told his story to their children and grandchildren. They had seen with their own eyes how Phaeton, the shining one, drove Apollo's horses, the day when the sun fell.

But in after years, children thought that the adventure of Phaeton was only a story of once upon a time, and they were not afraid.

Finn's Men and the Mean Mare

IN THE DAYS when Cormac was high king of Ireland, the chief captain of his fighting men was Finn MacCool of the Fair Hair. Finn's men lived a fine life, each with a house and land of his own, each with his own horses and hounds, so that the best men in Ireland gathered around him. They took a proud name for themselves, the Fianna, but the honour of being one of the Fianna was hard-earned, for it was the duty of Finn's men to keep the peace in the kingdom and to guard the coasts from seafarers who often landed to rob and plunder. Such was the service of the Fianna to the high king of Ireland.

Now each year when the harvest was in, Finn celebrated with a banquet in his castle on the Hill of Allen, where he would pick up his harp and sing of high deeds and adventures, for he was a great poet as well as a fighting man. Afterwards he would go to hunt with the Fianna. One year the hunt rode over hill and

dale westward across the plains of Munster, and on a certain day at All-Hallowtide they made camp on a hilltop within sight of the sea, putting their horses to graze. Finn sat down to watch the hunt with his captains around him, Dermot of the Love Spot, Liagan the Swift, Conan the Bald, who had the sharpest tongue, and a dozen others. While they were listening for the cry of the hounds and the sound of the hunting horn from the woods and fields below, an armed man came out of the woods and began to climb the hill, pulling a big, yellow-coated mare behind him at the end of a rope.

The man was huge, with tangled yellow hair and a broad red face as flat and ugly as if the mare had stepped on it. Everything about him was crooked: arms, shoulders, legs, teeth. Even his walk was crooked as he pulled the mare this way and that to make her go. When she would not go, he beat her sides with an iron club as a man beats a bass drum. The mare was as ugly as the man, her ribs showing through her rough flea-bitten coat, and her long back as sharp as the ridgepole of a house. Her knees were knobby. Sometimes she stumbled a few steps forward as the man tugged, sometimes she gave a shrill neigh like a scream and pulled him back, so that it was a long time before the two reached Finn and his men on the hilltop.

There the stranger bowed his knee and asked, "You are Finn MacCool?"

"I am," said Finn.

"I have come to serve as one of your horsemen," said the stranger. "I hear you will give work to any man who asks."

"So I do," said Finn. "And what may your name be?"

"That I don't know, for I never knew my father or mother, but I am called the Hard Servant. I am hard to get along with and I do nothing unless I have a mind to do it. My mare is the same."

Finn laughed. "At least you are honest. You don't praise yourself, which is a thing I never like. What wages do you want?"

"I will tell you that at the end of a year," said the Hard Servant. "Now let my mare graze among your horses."

He dropped the rope, and off shambled the yellow mare to the field where Finn's men put their horses to pasture. But the mare had no intention of grazing. She went among the fine horses of the Fianna like a devil, kicking one in the legs, biting another on the ear, all the time screaming like a mad thing, until the others screamed too and plunged about, while the hounds barked and the men shouted.

"Take that mare away!" Finn ordered.

But the Hard Servant answered, "I'm no horseboy, nor will I do a horseboy's work."

Then Conan the Bald ran forward in a rage and took the mare's halter in his hand, roaring, "I should beat out your brains and those of your mean mare, too." He tugged at the rope with all his might, but the mare would not move.

"Mount her," called Finn, "and gallop her till she drops. That will pay her for the damage she has done."

Conan threw a leg over the mare's back and

dug his heels into her sides, but she did not budge.

The Hard Servant jeered, "She does not know you're there. She wants a weight like mine on her back before she'll move."

So another of Finn's captains climbed up behind Conan the Bald. The mare stood stock still. Then another and another of the Fianna jumped on her back until fourteen men were astride her, while the rest doubled over with laughter to see such a sight.

The Hard Servant glowered, "You mock my mare, do you? Then I want no service with you, Finn MacCool. I'll go, and take my mare away." With that he stomped off down the hill, and the mare stumbled after him. Still laughing, the rest of the Fianna were making ready to join the hunt in the valley below when they heard Conan calling from halfway down the hill. "Help, Finn! We can't get down from this mare and she won't stop!"

And there was the ugly man, going at a run now, and the mare following at a canter, while the fourteen on her back thumped up and down with the pounding of the hoofs under them.

Conan shouted again, "Rescue, Finn!"

And Finn shouted back, "Rescue!" for he and his men were pledged to come to one another's aid in time of need. So off they all pelted after the mare, Liagan the Swift running first, up hill and down dale, through rivers and over rocks, until they came to the sea, where surely the ugly man and his long mare must stop. But not at all. Both man and mare plunged into the water just as Liagan got hold of her tail and was pulled along after her, for he could not let go of the tail any more than the fourteen could get free from the mare's back. When Finn and the rest of his captains reached the shore, man, mare, riders, and Liagan were well nigh out of sight. But Finn marked their direction, and all set to work to cut down trees and build a raft. Then with sails made from their cloaks, they put out to sea.

At the days end they reached an island they had never seen before, ringed round with sheer cliffs that dropped to a narrow beach. Here they landed, and Finn said, "There is some enchantment in this. I think there is no such island off the coast of Munster. And now I remember that it is All-Hallowtide, when the gates stand open between the Other World and ours, and there are comings and goings. All the more we must rescue our friends. This island does not welcome us, but let us sleep now, and tomorrow we will make a rope ladder to go up the cliff."

The next morning they began to make their ladder. But Dermot cried, "Too slow! To the rescue! Follow me!" Then the hero light blazed from him, and, taking a run, with his spear for a pole he vaulted to the top of the cliff and disappeared. Finn was the only other hero who could have made such a leap, but his duty was to stay with his men. When the ladder was finished, he made a noose at the end of the rope and with a mighty throw hurled it over a high pinnacle of rock. Then he and his men climbed the cliff, but they had no sight of Dermot.

Dermot had gone searching for the Hard Servant and the ugly mare who had stolen away his friends. He passed through rolling meadows bright with flowers and through fair woodlands, until he came to a bubbling spring of clear water so deep that he could not see to the bottom of it. Being thirsty, he bent down to drink.

Then the water of the spring stirred and murmured, and Dermot saw a warrior advancing through the woods. "Who gave you leave to roam my land and drink from my spring?" the warrior asked with angry looks, and drawing his sword, he challenged Dermot to battle. Dermot drew his own sword and they fought all that day, giving and taking hard blows. But as night fell, and the Warrior of the Spring saw that Dermot was about to overcome him, he dived into the water and was gone, so that Dermot thought he was drowned.

The second day, Dermot walked far, looking for the mare, until a great thirst came upon him and again he went to the spring and drank. Then once more the water moved and made a threatening sound. And once more the strange warrior came with drawn sword to do battle. Then Dermot said to himself, "This is enchantment. I am fighting against one of the Fair Folk, who cannot easily be defeated." But all the powers of Faerie could not overcome a hero of the Fianna, and once again as darkness came, the Warrior of the Spring leaped into the water and disappeared.

On the third day, after a long, hard hunt for the yellow mare, Dermot quenched his thirst at the spring, and the warrior came shouting, "Will you not be gone?" Then he rushed at Dermot to run him through with his sword.

Dermot answered, "I will not be gone until I rescue my comrades." And once again he proved himself the better swordsman. But this time, when the Warrior of the Spring turned to leap into the water, Dermot clutched him in both arms and sank down with him.

At first the light from above glimmered through the water. Then as they sank down, down, deeper and deeper, all became dim and full of shadows, and Dermot fell into a sleep. When he woke, he was lying in a grove of trees with golden branches and leaves of silver sparkling in rainbow light. Beyond the trees, fine horses of all colours were grazing or running free in a wide green flowery plain, and Dermot guessed that he was in Land-Under-Wave. He wondered whether he would find the ugly mare among those beautiful horses.

Then he saw riding towards him a champion with the look of god, so handsome was he. Yet his face was like that of the Warrior of the Spring, too, only kind instead of angry. He rode a mare, her coat as smooth as white silk, her white mane tossing like sea-foam. She was saddled in gold, with silver bells on the bridle rein. Dermot leaped to his feet and drew his sword. But the rider said, "A hundred thousand welcomes to you, Dermot. Finn himself has come to fight at my side. Now that you are come, I have all of Finn's captains with me, and you are the best of them."

"Who are you?" asked Dermot in awe, "and against whom do you fight? For I think this is Land-Under-Wave, and you are no Irishman, but one of the Fair Folk."

"You have guessed right," answered the champion on the white horse. "I am king of Faerie here. I fight against my brother, the warrior who fought against you at the spring. He would be king in my place if he could. When you came down with him into Land-Under-Wave, he left you lying here for dead. But it is no easy thing to kill a man of the Fianna. That is why I have brought Finn and his captains to fight for me. I met them at the top of the cliff above the beach and brought them down to my palace by a secret path. They are waiting for you now."

"And where are those who rode the yellow mare?" asked Dermot. "They are the ones we came to rescue."

"They are with Finn too," said the king. Then he reached out a hand to Dermot and said, "Come up behind me. You know me and my mare."

"Not I," said Dermot, looking in wonder at the royal champion and his white steed. "I never saw either of you before."

"Look again," said the king. And for a moment, as if a wave had passed over him, he had the face of the Hard Servant. He touched the white mare on the shoulder and said, "Show your earth shape." The mare trembled until the bridle bells jingled. She gave a shrill neigh, rearing up on her hind legs, and for an instant, only an instant, Dermot saw before his eyes, like a sea wave breaking on a beach of rock and sand, a yellow mare with a rough coat and a long, bony back. Then she was a beautiful white mare again, and Dermot swung himself up on her back behind the king of Land-Under-Wave.

Dermot never had such a ride. The white mare seemed to fly, so smoothly did she gallop through the sea-green meadows where the horses of Faerie grazed and ran. And all at once Dermot saw before him the king's palace, the beauty of its white walls rising from a hill among apple trees covered with blossoms of silver and fruit of gold. The high king of Ireland had not so fair a palace. And at the gates Dermot saw his comrades, those who had ridden the mare, Liagan the Swift, who had held her tail, Finn MacCool himself, and all who had sailed with him. The champions of Land-Under-Wave were at war games with them, on foot and in shining chariots, and from the windows of the palace highborn ladies, clad in mantles of green, watched the play of swords and spears. All welcomed Dermot with joy.

But there was little time to rejoice, for now came the king's wrathful brother at the head of his hosts of warriors, and the two armies formed battle lines. Yet the army of the king's brother turned pale when they saw Finn's men. Then Dermot stepped forward and called out to the king's brother, "You, Warrior of the Spring, I have fought you three times when we were alone. Stand forth and face me in single combat, so that we may prove our mettle in the sight of all. Let your quarrel with the king of this Land-Under-Wave be settled by our fight."

The king's brother grasped his spear and drew his sword and came to meet Dermot. Then such blows and thrusts were given and taken as none had ever seen. The combat of the two was

like the surging of waves in a gale, seething and
booming and bursting with the crack of
thunderbolts against a rock coast, while the
armies shook their spears and raised the war cry
for their champions. Just so, the wind shrieks
and howls when the sea rages. But the king's
brother was not able to strike down the best of
Finn's men, and at last, falling to his knees, he
admitted defeat. Because he was one of the Fair
Folk, he could not be killed but went off with his
followers, plotting revenge in his dark mind if
he ever found the king without Finn's men at
his side.

"Yes, he will come again," said the king.
"And you, Finn, will come again when I need
you, for I have often come to your aid."

"When did you come?" asked Finn.

"You did not see me as you see me here, but I
have always been with you in victory as my
brother was with you in defeat. We are the luck
of Ireland, Finn, the good luck and the bad.
And now that you have served me in your turn,
what wages do you ask?"

Finn laughed. "I paid you nothing when you
took service with me. You owe me nothing for
my service to you."

"Take this then for remembrance," said the
king, and he broke off a silver twig from the
branch of an apple tree and gave it to Finn.

All of the captains were content except for
Conan, who grumbled, "I am still sore from my
ride on that misbegotten mare. Something is
owed me for that."

"What would you have?" asked the king.

"A ride home on a white horse the equal of

yours," said Conan, "and the same for Finn and for each of us. And let fourteen of your captains ride that mean mare to Erin with you hanging onto the tail."

"Done," said the king. "Wait for us at the Hill of Allen."

And in the twinkling of an eye, Finn and his men found themselves each astride a white horse with a mane like blown sea spray, riding, riding the crests of the waves, galloping up the beach of Munster, flying over rocks and rivers, down dale and up hill to Finn's castle on the Hill of Allen. There they put the white horses to graze and sat down to wait for the king of Land-Under-Wave and his captains.

If they came, the Fianna never saw them, for they could not sit long. There were always brave deeds to be done in service to the high king of Ireland. But this much the Fianna knew: Sometimes they had good luck and sometimes bad, especially at All-Hallowtide when the gates were open between the Other World and this one. Then Finn would strike his harp and sing of Land-Under-Wave:

> *"I bring a branch of* Evin's *apple tree*
> *In shape alike to those you know:*
> *Twigs of white silver are upon it,*
> *Buds of crystal with blossoms.*

> *"There is a distant isle,*
> *Around which sea horses glisten . . .*
> *A delight of the eyes, a glorious range*
> *Is the plain on which the hosts hold games.*

"Fairest land throughout the world,
On which the many blossoms drop.
The sea washes the waves against the land,
A crystal spray drops from its mane.

"Golden chariots on the plain of the sea
Heaving with the tide to the sun:
Chariots of silver on the Plain of Sports,
And of bronze that has no blemish.

"There are thrice fifty distant isles
In the ocean to the west of us:
Larger than Erin twice
Is each of them, or thrice."

The Horse Who Built the Wall

Once the king of Sweden disguised himself as an old man and went to Asgard, the home of the gods, to find out why things are as they are. This is what the gods told him, a story both true and untrue, which was afterwards set down in the Grandmother Tales of the far northern lands.

IN THE BEGINNING, before heaven and earth were created, there was nothing but space, deep, black, empty, and cold. True and untrue, for south of the cold was a world of light and heat, glowing and burning, and in the darkness floated a mist that became water, dropping into the great gulf. The water formed into layer upon layer of ice, until the dark abyss was filled.

Then out of the ice came a frost giant, huge, grim, and dull-witted, and after him other giants who did nothing good. True and untrue, for strangely it was from the race of giants that the mighty god Odin came at last, full of

35

wisdom and beauty. He and his brothers smashed the oldest of the frost giants into bits, and from the pieces of his body they made the world.

The giant's flesh became earth, his blood the seas, his bones the mountain crags. Of the giant's hair the gods made trees. His skull they set over the earth as a great airy dome to hold the heavens in place. His dim brain became clouds. Then from embers and sparks of the southern fire Odin shaped the sun and the moon and tossed them into the sky. In that light plants and animals came to life on earth.

Still the work of creation was not finished. From the tough wood of an ash tree Odin made the first man. From a graceful elm tree he made the first woman, and the man and the woman called him All-father. He gave them the world for a home where they could live with their children and grandchildren, and a home for those who would come after them. Odin called their world Midgard, and he made the eyebrows of the oldest giant into a wall to keep his people safe. But even within the circle of the wall the people were not safe, for in time there came to be hill giants, called trolls, in the mountains of Midgard, and beyond the wall there were still frost giants who might someday break through.

Yet the gods had done all they could for Midgard. Now they began to build a city for themselves above the earth. First they built a great golden hall so high in the clouds that the top could not easily be seen. There was Odin's high seat where he sat in judgment with all the gods and goddesses around him. They built palaces of gold and silver and a hall for heroes who had fallen in battle on earth. Its roof was thatched with golden shields. From Midgard men could see only the gleam of the shining towers that lit the sky at sunset, but these glimpses of the heavenly city, Asgard, assured them that the gods were watching over them.

A rainbow bridge led from Midgard to Asgard, though no mortal had ever found the lower end of it, and besides, a watchman guarded the top of the bridge with eyes so sharp that he could see by night as well as by day. His ears were so keen that he could hear the grass growing. Yet even their watchman did not make the gods feel safe in Asgard. One more thing was needed, a wall around the city to turn it into a fortress. The gods met in council to plan how such a wall might be built but could decide nothing.

Soon after this a stranger came up the rainbow bridge. He had broad shoulders and heavily muscled arms. He seemed to be an ordinary workman and was carrying a bag of tools. The watchman at the bridge blew on his golden horn a blast that brought all the gods in Asgard to the bridgehead, armed with swords and spears. Only Thor was absent. He, the strongest of all the gods, had gone with his thunderbolt hammer to fight trolls at the ends of the earth.

As the stranger came near, Odin called out, "Who are you, and what do you want?"

"I am a stonemason," answered the stranger. "I have come to build a wall around Asgard so strong and high that the gods can live behind it safely forever and ever."

"What is the price?" asked Loki, suspiciously.

Now Loki was not a god. He was part troll, a trickster, a shape-changer, and a troublemaker, who lived for the pleasure of working his will on others. But he was handsome and clever and liked to undo mischief as well as to make it, so the gods let him stay in Asgard.

"The price?" said the stonemason. "Only the sun and the moon and the goddess Freya."

The gods were troubled when they heard this answer. Without the sun and the moon, the old darkness and cold would return, and all things on earth would die. As for Freya, she was the goddess of love, whose beauty filled the gods with delight. Without her, Asgard would lose its joy, and without joy the gods too might as well die. Yet they did need a wall.

"When could you finish the work?" asked Odin.

"I would need two winters and the summer between," said the stranger. "You will never have a better offer. What do you say? The sun and the moon and the goddess Freya in exchange for the safety of Asgard."

"You drive a hard bargain," answered Loki. "Come back when we have had time to think about this."

Loki waited until the stonemason had gone down the rainbow bridge. Then he said, "Let us agree to his terms. Only tell him that he must finish the wall in one winter and put the last stone in place before the first day of summer. And he must do all the work himself with no other man's help. He is greedy and will try with all his might, but, strong as he is, he will not succeed. So we will have part of our wall built without cost and will keep the sun and the moon and the goddess Freya."

Odin did not like tricks, but since none of the gods could think of a better plan, they decided to take Loki's advice.

When the stonemason returned and heard the terms of the bargain, he frowned. Then he looked at Freya with longing and said, "Very well. I will finish the wall by the first day of summer and I will do the work with the help of no man. Otherwise you need not pay me. Only allow me to bring my old horse," he said. "Surely you cannot object to that."

Loki thought there could be no harm in an old horse, so again the gods agreed and swore an oath to keep their part of the bargain.

On the first day of winter the stonemason came with his horse, and at sight of the horse the gods wondered. He was a black stallion. Though he might be old, the muscles of his great neck and shoulders rippled under a hide that looked too tough and thick for any sword to cut, and the rainbow bridge trembled under his weight.

At the edge of Asgard the stonemason unpacked his tools and began to work. He toiled mightily all through the short winter day, and when the long night came, the horse worked, hauling stones as big as mountains for the mason to cut and fit the next day. No load was too heavy for the stallion, no distance too far. He seemed to have no desire except work. Patiently, tirelessly, he pulled the great weight of the stones while all Asgard shook with the thunder of the enormous hoofs that never slipped on ice or snow.

Through the long winter nights the horse hauled so many stones and the wall rose so fast that the gods began to be afraid. On the third day before the end of winter only the gateway remained to be built. Then all of the gods and goddesses came into the great hall of Asgard where Odin sat in his high seat.

"Who thought of the plan to trick the stone-mason?" they said. "He must be no ordinary workman but a giant in disguise. It was you, Loki, who persuaded us to risk losing our greatest treasures. It was you who said that the stonemason could bring his horse. Now we see that the horse does most of the work. Without him the workman could have done nothing. Now because of you we are in the worst danger we have ever known. You deserve to die a thousand deaths."

But Loki hid his fear and said, "Leave it to me. I give you my oath that the builder shall lose his wages, no matter what it costs me."

On the last night of winter the moon shone very round and bright. Only a few stones were missing at the top of the gateway, and the stonemason and his horse were labouring harder than ever, when out of a woods nearby, a pretty white mare came running. She whinnied to the stallion and, frisking up her heels, ran back into the woods. The great horse stopped his work and stood stock still. Then he tore loose from his harness and galloped into the woods after the mare. At this, the stonemason dropped his disguise and appeared in his true form as a giant troll, shouting curses and running after the horse, storming and howling in fury. All night he raged around Asgard while he searched for his stallion, but in vain.

When All-father saw how the giant trolls had deceived the gods, he ordered the trumpeter to blow his golden horn for the return of Thor from the ends of the earth. With the speed of lightning and a roll of thunder Thor came, hammer in hand. He hurled his weapon at the giant and split his skull into stony splinters that went spinning off into outer space.

The danger was not past. Always at the top of Asgard's gateway three stones were missing, so that the gods were never completely safe from the giants. But the goddess Freya gave them joy even in danger, and the sun and moon still shed their light on heaven and earth.

Neither the stallion nor the mare were seen again in Asgard, nor did Loki return for many months. When he did come, he brought with him a marvellous foal, a steed fit for the gods. It was grey and had eight legs on which it could gallop faster than light through air and water. Loki gave the horse to Odin, who found it to be the best of all the horses in Asgard, strong as the great stallion who had built the wall, graceful as the mare who had led the stallion into the woods on the last night of winter. Loki would not tell where he had found the grey horse. He would only say, "Am I not Loki, the shape-changer?" Then he would give a laugh that sounded rather like a whinny.

This is only one of the stories, true and untrue, that the gods told to the king of Sweden when he went to Asgard. Since then, no man has set foot on the rainbow bridge, and the gods have told no more about why things are as they are.

Pecos Bill's Widow-Maker

YOU'RE ASKING did I ever see Pecos Bill? See him myself? Well, yes and no. I mean, I'm not *that* old. Pecos Bill showed up in the West about the time there began to be cowboys, and that's more than a hundred years ago. You might say he's the granddaddy of all the cowboys you see today. But then again, I've seen *your* granddaddy, knew him well. Every time I look at you, I can see him. And every time I see a cowboy at a rodeo, I'm seeing Pecos Bill, because he taught them everything they know. To tell you the truth, I don't think he's dead yet. If he had been dead, famous as he is, there would have been headlines in all the papers, wouldn't there? So he must be out there still, if you looked for him in the right places. Of course that would mean a fair-sized piece of real estate, from Texas up through Montana on both sides of the Rockies. You could skip the cities and all around the motorways and head on into the prairies where

it's wide and empty, but it would still be some search.

They say Bill's ma and pa were looking for a wide empty place when Bill got born. The family kept moving west every time they'd see smoke going up from a chimney not far away. It gave them a smothery feeling to have any folks so close. So they'd put all the children in the old covered wagon and go on again. I don't know just where Bill was born. Maybe in that covered wagon, or maybe in a little old sod hut somewhere in Texas. I heard his ma fed him panther milk and let him cut his teeth on a bowie knife. Anyway, he must have been a knee baby by the time they got to the Pecos River, and he was sound asleep in the very back of the wagon when a rear wheel hit a stone, and he fell out. His pa and ma didn't even know he was missing till she made some flapjacks a couple of weeks later and passed them out, twelve for every child. There was one pile left over, and that's when they noticed Bill was gone.

They went back a good piece, but they never found him, and his ma said, "I'll bet he fell out when we hit that stone at the Pecos River." So that's why they called him Pecos Bill when they talked about him—Pecos for the river, and Bill because it sounded good.

They never would have found him, because he had gone off with an old coyote. I've heard it was the same one that brought fire to the Indians and showed them how to keep warm and to cook. He took Bill back to his cave and taught him to keep alive on the prairie and find something to eat and water to drink any time of year, no matter how hot or how cold, and to keep going all day without a rest, and to sleep on the ground at night. He taught Bill to howl, too.

So Bill grew up thinking he was a coyote. You'd never believe how big he grew. He had wide shoulders and narrow hips and long legs. The soles of his feet were hard and tough like a coyote's, and his toes had claws, which are a lot more useful than toenails when it comes to living on the prairie. All that time he never wore any clothes or saw a human being, only animals —buffalo, and wild cattle and horses and such. He could talk to any kind of animals in their own language, even mountain lions and snakes, when he got near enough to hear how they talked. Naturally, he was very good at talking to coyotes, and they liked him a lot. When food was scarce, Bill would go off and catch a wild steer by the tail. Then he would kill it with his bare hands and take it home so the coyotes could have a good meal.

How did Bill find out he wasn't a coyote? Well, about the time he was grown, there started to be cowboys out West, and Bill would make himself invisible and listen to them talking at night around a campfire. He got so he could talk the same way they did, only better. Then one day when he got good and ready, he came right up to a cowboy who was on his horse, watering a few cattle at a river. The cowboy was scared half to death when he saw how big Bill was.

"Who are you?" he asked, with his teeth chattering.

"I'm a coyote," said Pecos Bill.

"No, you're not," said the cowboy. "You're a man. Where are your clothes?"

"Coyotes don't wear clothes," Pecos Bill told him.

"Here are two blankets," the cowboy said. "Make yourself some pants."

So Bill decided to look at himself in the river and find out whether he was a coyote or a man. When he found out he was a man, he thought he'd throw in with humans, so he took the two blankets and made himself a shirt. Then he laid hold of an old steer's tail and yelled "Yee-ow!" like a wild coyote, and that steer was so scared he jumped right out of his skin. Pecos Bill took the hide and made himself some cowboy chaps. They were the first ones, and Bill invented them. He wouldn't have done it if it had been winter, because it took the steer six weeks to grow a new hide. Bill was kind—tough kind.

How did he find out he was the Pecos Bill that had fallen out of the wagon? To tell the truth, I don't know, and I aim to tell nothing but the truth. Just keep still and listen.

So he said good-bye to the coyotes and went off with Smitty—that was the name of the cowboy—to the ranch where he worked, and Smitty helped him get some clothes that fitted, and a hat. The other cowboys all wore ten-gallon hats, but Pecos Bill had to wear a forty-gallon hat. He got some boots, too. Cowboys wore tight boots to make their feet look small, and Bill hated those boots. Whenever he could, he'd take them off and go bare-foot. That way he could run faster than any horse.

Of course, Pecos Bill had learned to ride a

bronco the very first day at the ranch, but he never needed to own one. He just rode to show the cowboys how to rope a steer from the saddle and then jump off and hogtie it. They never could do that before Bill came. And no one could break a bronco the way he could. He'd take off his boots and jump on the back of the wild animal. Then he'd get a grip on the mane and dig in with the claws on his toes. That bronco could try bucking and cakewalking— that's when he tilts backward on his hind legs— and corkscrewing and high diving, but Bill would hang on until the horse quieted down and gave up so he could be saddled and bridled.

One thing Bill found out right away at the ranch was that the cowboys didn't do much work. They'd take the cattle to water or pasture, but the rest of the time they mostly sat around the ranch chewing tobacco and telling lies about how great they were. They were supposed to catch wild cattle and bring them back to the herd, but the best they could do was to spread a noose on the prairie and hope an animal would walk into it. Cattle were always wandering off, too, and getting lost, so the herds stayed pretty puny. But Pecos Bill changed all that. He knew the prairies were full of wild cattle just waiting to be caught. So he thought about it for a while, and then he came up with a new invention. He got a couple of old steer hides the same way I told you, and he made them into one long, thin strip with a noose at the end. It was the first lariat, and Bill started practicing how to throw it, until he could rope in anything he aimed at. After a while, all cowboys had lariats. None of them could bring down an animal as fast as Bill could, but pretty soon the herds began to grow. Then Bill had a better idea. He made a lariat long enough to go around the world, and when he saw a big herd of cattle, he'd rope the whole lot of them with one throw and bring them on back to the ranch.

A big problem in those days was telling whose cattle were whose. Herds would get mixed up on the range, and cowboys from different ranches would start shooting each other for stealing. Well, Pecos Bill showed the ranch blacksmith how to make a branding iron, and it wasn't long before all the ranchers were branding their cattle. It wasn't much fun for the cattle, but you can see it was better in the long run.

Then Pecos Bill said to the men, "This is a whole new kind of cowpunching. Starting now, we're going to ride all day long to keep the herd together, and we've got to take turns riding the herd all night too. When we aren't riding at night, we'll sleep on the ground. We won't be eating at the ranch much, either. We'll eat from a chuck wagon that will go right along with us on the range. In the spring we'll have a big roundup, and then we'll ride herd along the trail to market. And we're really going to look after the dogies." What are dogies? They're poor little motherless calves.

Well, at first the men said this sounded too much like work. But Pecos Bill said, "You've been telling lies all along about how great you were. Now you're going to *be* great." Then he went off all over the West to show cowboys how to work, and they have been great ever since.

As I said, Bill never had wanted a horse of his own because he could outrun any horse he had ever seen. But to make travelling easy he tamed a mountain lion and put a saddle and bridle on it. You should have seen them, Bill whooping and yelling and waving his hat, and the mountain lion going thirty metres at every jump. Bill tamed a rattlesnake, too, and looped it over his saddle horn. When he made it whip around, it was the best quirt a cowboy ever had.

It must have been when Bill was off on his travels that he heard about a great pacing white stallion. A pacer puts his two left feet forward at the same time and then his two right feet, which is the easiest and smoothest way a horse can go. Bill heard that this white stallion was the biggest and fastest and most beautiful horse in the world, with a whole herd of pretty mares following after him. Some cowboys said they didn't believe there was any such animal, because if there was, it would have to have been sired by the flying horse with wings in the story thousands of years ago. But finally Bill met some cowboys who claimed they had seen the horse, so Bill made up his mind to find him. The men said they had tried to catch him the best way it could be done. Each man had a string of horses and covered all the trails around every time they'd catch sight of the stallion. But they couldn't any more than just keep him in sight, even though they changed to fresh horses all the time and ran those horses till they dropped. They went on chasing him for a week, and the stallion never even changed his pace.

When Pecos Bill heard this, he wanted to see the white horse more than he had ever wanted anything, but it took him about two years of travelling, from the Southwest clear out to the Pacific Coast and way up into Canada.

Then one night he camped in the Crazy Mountains. You think I'm joking? Look them up on the map. They're there, in Montana. Anyway, in the morning Bill thought he saw the sun coming up with a white cloud on each side of it. When he looked again, he saw it was a horse, not white like they had told him, but a palomino, pale gold with a white mane and a white tail, and Pecos Bill knew this was the horse he had been looking for. He gave a neigh you could hear to Kingdom Come, and he heard an answer. He didn't know if it was his own voice echoing in the mountains or the neigh of the palomino, far off, like a bugle call. Then he saw the horse was coming towards him, and he made himself invisible for a while, but neighing all the time, until the stallion came up right beside him, head and tail up, looking proud and free.

Bill made himself visible again and started to talk in horse language as nice as could be. But the palomino was suspicious. He shied and snorted, and Bill saw he was going to run, so he threw his lariat right over that sleek neck. Then he pulled back and dug in his heels, but the stallion reared up and came down with his front hoofs so hard and sharp that the leather snapped in two. He shook off the noose and went like a streak of greased lightning with Bill after him. They covered the West from Montana to

Mexico and back again before Bill got the palomino cornered in a gulch and did a flipflop onto his back, landing face forward. That's quite a trick, and you can still see cowboys do it in a rodeo. Bill taught them.

Anyway, before he could get hold with his hands or toes, the stallion arched his back so high and fast that Bill went several kilometres into the air. He came down wedged between some jagged rocks like a pickle in the top of a pickle bottle. This saved his life, because those rocks were so sharp they could have speared him like a pickle fork. But he pulled himself together and saw the palomino right below him, standing still, waiting to find out if Bill was gone for good. Bill dropped straight down on the stallion's back, and this time he got a good grip with both hands in the thick mane. He dug his claws into the ribs and hung on tight with his knees.

Well, the stallion tried every way in the world to throw Bill off. He corkscrewed and cake-walked and reared high up—that's what they call "skyscraping"—and jumped a kilometre back and two kilometres forwards, but Bill hung on. The stallion had one more trick, crashing down to earth on his back to crush his rider under him. But Bill had a trick to match that one. He slid out before the horse landed. Then he sat down on the neck, putting his heels on the cheek. The harder the palomino struggled, the harder Bill came down on the cheek, and at the same time he started to sweet-talk the horse, patting him on the shoulder and stroking his nose. Bill said that he was the greatest cowboy of all time and he wanted the greatest horse that ever lived to be his partner and help him make the American West the greatest cattle country in the world.

The palomino started to listen. Bill promised he would never try to break his spirit, because he was wild and free himself and he wouldn't want his horse to be any other way. Then, to show he was telling the truth, he got up and walked off a way, leaving the horse to decide what he wanted to do. The palomino leaped to his feet and stood for a few minutes, trying to make up his mind. Then he went and nuzzled Bill's shoulder.

When Bill came back to the ranch riding the palomino, the eyes of the other cowboys popped out. They couldn't believe what they were seeing, especially when Bill jumped down and the horse stayed by his shoulder.

Smitty said, "I want to ride that horse just once, Bill."

"Better not," Bill said.

But Smitty wouldn't take no for an answer. He made a run and landed on the palomino's back. Well, he didn't stay there long. A second later he was up in the air and out of sight. The other cowboys had to ask around for quite a spell to find out if he had landed somewhere, and finally they heard he was up on top of Pike's Peak and couldn't get down. So Pecos Bill shook out his lariat and threw. He caught Smitty around the middle and tightened the noose. Then he pulled him in. You should have seen Smitty. Every bone in his body was broken. The cowboys couldn't help feeling sorry for him, even though it was his own fault, so Bill laid him out straight in his bunk with all his bones back in place, and in about two weeks he was in perfect shape again. He thanked Pecos Bill for saving his life and asked, "Bill, has that horse got a name?"

"Not that I know of," Bill answered.

"Well, then," said Smitty, "call him Widow-Maker."

So that's how Bill's famous horse got his name.

From then on, nothing could stop the American West from being the greatest cattle country in the world, because Pecos Bill and Widow-Maker were in charge of everything.

You'd think Bill would have been perfectly happy now that he had Widow-Maker, but sometimes he got pretty lonely out on the prairie, just the way the other cowboys did, so he taught them songs to quiet the cattle or sing around the campfire at night. Pecos Bill wrote all the cowboy songs. One of them was:

"I'm a poor lonesome cowboy,
I'm a poor lonesome cowboy,
I'm a poor lonesome cowboy,
And a long way from home."

It was easy to learn and all the cowboys sang it. It sounded nice and sad, sort of like a bunch of coyotes howling, especially when one cowboy would play the tune on a mouth organ. The song went on:

"I ain't got no father,

I ain't got no mother,
No sister and no brother
To ride along with me.

"I ain't got no sweetheart,
I ain't got no sweetheart,
I ain't got no sweetheart
To sit and talk with me."

Pecos Bill got to wishing he had a sweetheart, but there were no ladies on the range, and the girls in the cowtowns were no ladies, either. Anyway, not too many cowboys got married. They didn't want to be hogtied by a woman. But one day when Bill was down on the Rio Grande, he saw a pretty girl riding a catfish, with just a girth cinched around it for her to hold on by. And those catfish in the Rio Grande are bigger than Whales. That got Bill interested, so he asked around and found out that she lived on a dude ranch where tender-foots, people from the East, could come and pretend to be cowboys for a summer. The girl's name was Slue-foot Sue and she helped her ma and her pa run the ranch. They called her Slue-foot because she could dance and kick up her heels and twirl around better than any other girl when they started square dancing at a hoedown. She had her own horse, too, and when she was riding in her buckskin shirt and chaps and wearing a sombrero, she was the best-looking cowboy that ever wore spurs, except of course she was a cowgirl.

Bill was almost too bashful to speak to her, but she helped him out. She kept looking at him and singing to him:

> "As I was a-walkin' one morning for pleasure
> I spied a cowpuncher a-ridin' along;
> His hat was throwed back and his spurs was
>   a-jinglin',
> And as he approached he was singin' this song–
> 'Whoopee ti yi yo, git along, little dogies,
> It's your misfortune and none of my own,
> Whoopee ti yi yo, git along, little dogies,
> For you know Wyoming will be your new
>   home.'"

From this Bill got the idea that Slue-foot Sue liked him, too, and since she liked everything else he liked, he finally got up his nerve to ask her to marry him. She said yes right away.

Well, everything went along fine till the wedding. That day Sue wore a white silk dress with a steel-spring bustle that was all the style, and she looked as pretty as a picture. After the wedding she said, "Oh, Bill, you said you loved me. Will you promise me one thing?"

"Why, sure," Bill said. "Anything you want, Sue." He was plain loco about her.

"Whoopee!" said Sue. "Let me ride Widow-Maker!"

"You can't do that!" Bill told her, and he explained what had happened when Smitty tried to ride the stallion.

"You promised!" Sue yelled. And with that she jumped on the back of the palomino. Well, the next minute she was up in the sky, and when she came down again, she landed on the steel-spring bustle and bounced up again as high as the moon. In fact, she had to dodge to keep from hitting it. What was worse, she kept on bouncing up and down for about a week, until Bill finally got where she was coming down and caught her. After that, Slue-foot Sue didn't ask to ride Widow-Maker any more, and she and Bill got along fine.

What do I think happened to them? Well, it stands to reason that Pecos Bill would have found a good place to live, smart as he was and knowing every bit of every state all over the West. So I think he must have found a nice valley that nobody else knew about, where it never snowed and never got too hot either, and where there was plenty of water and green grass for Widow-Maker and his herd of mares. And Bill and Sue would have had enough children to help them run the best ranch in the West. Of course, after a while, they weren't so young anymore, but they didn't get old either, not so you could notice it. Widow-Maker? Well, he surely sired some beautiful colts and fillies, didn't he? Because if you go out West you can still see palominos with pale-gold coats and white manes and tails, and it's just like seeing the granddaddy of them all, Pecos Bill's Widow-Maker.

Falada and the Goosegirl

THERE WAS once upon a time an old queen whose husband had been dead for many years and she had a beautiful daughter. When the princess grew up she was to marry a prince who lived in another country, so before the wedding she had to journey forth into the distant kingdom. The aged queen packed up for her many plates and bowls of silver and gold, and jewels also, set in gold and silver, everything that was needed for a royal dowry, because she loved her child with all her heart.

She likewise sent her maid-in-waiting, who was to ride with the princess and hand her over to the bridegroom, and each had a horse for the journey, but the horse of the queen's daughter was called Falada and could speak.

When the hour of parting came, the aged mother went into her bedroom, took a small knife, and cut her finger with it. Then she let three drops of blood fall into a white hand-

kerchief and gave it to her daughter, saying, "Dear child, do not lose this. It will be of help to you on your way."

They took a sorrowful leave of each other, and the princess put the handkerchief in the bosom of her dress, mounted Falada, and rode away to meet her bridegroom. After she had ridden for a while she felt a burning thirst, and said to her waiting maid, "Dismount, if you please, and fill my golden cup with water from the stream, for I should like to drink."

"If you are thirsty," said the waiting maid, "get off your horse yourself and lie down and drink of the water. I don't choose to be your servant, and I will not allow you to drink out of the golden cup."

So, in her great thirst, the princess alighted, bent down over the water in the stream and drank. Then she said, "Ah, Heaven!" and the three drops of blood answered, "If this your mother knew, her heart would break in two." But the queen's daughter was humble, said nothing, and mounted Falada again. She rode on further, but the day was warm, the sun scorched her, and she was thirsty once more. So when they came to a stream of water, she again called to her waiting maid: "Dismount, please, and give me some water in my golden cup." But the waiting maid said still more haughtily than before, "If you wish to drink, get it yourself. I don't choose to be your maid."

Then in her great thirst the queen's daughter dismounted from Falada's back, bent over the flowing stream, wept, and said, "Ah Heaven!" And the drops of blood again replied, "If this your mother knew, her heart would break in two." And as she was thus drinking and leaning right over the stream, the handkerchief with the three drops of blood fell out of the bosom of her dress and floated away in the water without her noticing it, so great was her trouble.

The waiting maid, however, had seen it, and she rejoiced that she now had power over the bride, for since the princess had lost the drops of blood, she had become weak and powerless against the cruel girl. So now when the princess wanted to mount Falada again, the waiting maid said, "Falada is more suitable for me, and my nag will do for you," and the princess had to let her have her way. Then the waiting maid, with many hard words, bade the princess exchange her royal garments for her own plain clothes, and at length she compelled the princess to swear by the clear sky above her that she would not say one word of this to anyone at court, and if she had not taken the oath she would have been killed on the spot. But Falada saw everything and observed it well.

The waiting maid now mounted Falada and the true bride the other horse, and thus they travelled onward, until at length they came to the prince's palace. There were great rejoicings over their arrival, and the prince sprang forward to meet the waiting maid, lifted her from Falada's back, and thought she was his bride-to-be. She was led upstairs to the royal apartments, but the real princess was left standing below.

Then the old king looked out of the window and saw her standing in the courtyard and noticed how dainty and delicate and beautiful she was, and instantly he went to the royal apartments and asked the false bride about the girl she had with her who was standing down below in the courtyard. She answered, "I picked her up on my way for a companion. Give her something to work at, that she may not be idle."

The old king said, "She can go to the meadow. I have a little boy who tends the geese. She may help him." The boy was called Conrad, and the true bride had to go to help him tend the geese.

Soon afterwards, the false bride said to the prince, "Dearest husband, I beg you to do me a favour." He answered, "Most willingly, I will do whatever you ask."

"Then have the head of the horse on which I rode here cut off, for it annoyed me on the way."

The prince did not like this demand, but she said over and over that he had promised to do whatever she asked, and at last he ordered that it should be done. When it came to the ears of the real princess that the faithful Falada was to die, she secretly promised to pay a servant a piece of gold if he would perform a small service for her. There was a great dark gateway in the town wall, through which morning and evening she had to pass with the geese. She begged the servant to nail up Falada's head on it, so that she might see him again each day. The man promised to do that, and when Falada's head was cut off he nailed it above the dark gateway.

Early the next morning, when the princess and Conrad drove out their flock beneath this gateway, she said in passing:

> "*Faithful Falada, are you there?*"

Then the head answered:

> "*Alas, princess, how ill you fare!*
> *If this your mother knew,*
> *Her heart would break in two.*"

Then they went out of the town and drove their geese into the country. And when they had come to the meadow, the princess sat down and unbound her hair, which was like pure gold, and Conrad delighted in its brightness and wanted to have a bit of it for himself. But she said:

> "*Blow, gentle wind, I say,*
> *Blow Conrad's hat away,*
> *And make him chase it here and there,*
> *Till I have braided all my hair,*
> *And bound it up again.*"

And there came such a violent wind that it blew Conrad's hat away across country, and he was forced to run after it. When he came back she had finished combing her hair and was putting it up again, and he could not get at it. Then Conrad was angry and would not speak to her, and so they watched the geese until evening, and went home.

Next day when they were driving the geese out through the dark gateway, the princess said,

> "*Faithful Falada, are you there?*"

Falada answered,

> *"Alas, princess, how ill you fare!*
> *If this your mother knew,*
> *Her heart would break in two."*

And she sat down again in the field and began to comb her hair, and Conrad ran and tried to clutch it, so she said in haste:

> *"Blow, gentle wind, I say,*
> *Blow Conrad's hat away,*
> *And make him chase it here and there,*
> *Till I have braided all my hair,*
> *And bound it up again."*

Then the wind blew, and blew Conrad's little hat off his head and far away, and he was forced to run after it, and when he came back to the goosegirl, her hair had been put up a long time, and so they looked after their geese till evening came.

But after they had got home, Conrad went to the old king and said, "I won't tend the geese with that girl any longer!"

"Why not?" inquired the king.

"Oh, because she teases me the whole day long." Then the king commanded him to relate what it was that she did to him. And Conrad said, "In the morning when we pass beneath the dark gateway with the flock, there is a horse's head on the wall, and she says to it:

> *'Faithful Falada, are you there?'*

And the head replies:

> 'Alas, princess, how ill you fare!
> If this your mother knew,
> Her heart would break in two.' ''

And Conrad went on to relate what happened in the goose pasture and how he had to chase his hat.

The old king commanded him to drive his flock out again next day, and as soon as morning came, he placed himself behind the dark gateway and heard how the maiden spoke to the head of Falada, and then he, too, went into the country and hid himself in a thicket in the meadow. There he soon saw with his own eyes the goosegirl and the gooseboy bringing their flock, and how after a while she sat down and unbraided her hair, which shone with radiance. And soon she said:

> ''Blow, gentle wind, I say,
> Blow Conrad's hat away,
> And make him chase it here and there,
> Till I have braided all my hair,
> And bound it up again.''

Then came a blast of wind and carried off Conrad's hat, so that he had to run far away, while the maiden quietly went on combing and plaiting her hair. All of this the king observed. Then, quite unseen, he went away, and when the goosegirl came home in the evening, he called her aside and asked why she did all these things.

She answered, "I may not tell that, or tell my sorrows to any human being, for I have sworn not to do so by the heaven which is above me. If I had not done that, I should have lost my life."

He urged her and left her no peace, but he could draw nothing from her. Then said he, "If you will not tell me anything, tell your sorrows to the iron stove there," and he went away. Then she crept into the iron stove and began to weep and lament and emptied her whole heart and said, "Here am I deserted by all the world except my faithful Falada, and yet I am a king's daughter, and a false waiting maid has by force brought me to such a pass that I have been compelled to put off my royal dress, and she has taken my place with my bridegroom, while I have to do the work of goosegirl. If this my mother knew, her heart would break in two."

The old king, however, was standing outside by the stovepipe and was listening to what she said and took heed of everything. Then he came back to her again and bade her come out of the stove. And royal garments were put on her, and it was marvellous how beautiful she was!

The king summoned his son and revealed to him that he had got the false bride, who was only a waiting maid, but that the true bride, who had been the goosegirl, was standing there. The prince rejoiced with all his heart when he saw her beauty and youth, and a great feast was made ready to which all the people were invited. At the head of the table sat the bridegroom with the princess at one side of him in royal robes and the waiting maid on the other, but she did not recognize the princess in her dazzling array.

When they had eaten and drunk and were merry, the old king asked the waiting maid, as a riddle, what punishment a person deserved who had behaved in such and such a way and at the same time related the whole story and asked what sentence such a person should have.

Then the false bride said, "She deserves the worst that can be. She should be put to death."

"You have pronounced your own sentence," said the old king, "and thus you shall die." And when the sentence had been carried out, the prince married his true bride, and both of them reigned over their kingdom in peace and happiness.

Dapplegrim

ONCE ON A TIME there was a rich couple who had twelve sons, but the youngest, when he was grown up, said he would be off into the world to try his luck. His father and mother said he had better stay at home. But no, he couldn't rest, so at last they let him go. And when he had walked a good bit, he came to a king's palace where he asked for work and got it.

Now the king's daughter was his only child, and she had been stolen away by a troll who carried her off to his cave in a hill. So the king and all his people were in great grief and sorrow, and the king gave his word that anyone who could set the princess free should marry her and have half the kingdom. But there was no one who could do it, though many tried.

Now when the lad had been there a year or more, he longed to go home and see his father and mother. So back he went, but when he got home his father and mother were dead and his

brothers had divided up all that the old people owned, so there was nothing left for the lad.

"Who could tell you were still alive when you went gadding about so long?" said his brothers. "But there are twelve mares up in the field that we haven't yet shared among us. If you want them for your share, you're welcome."

So the lad thanked his brothers and went at once up to the field where the twelve mares were grazing. Each one of them had a foal at her side and one of them had a second foal, a big dapple grey, so sleek that the sun shone from his coat.

"A fine fellow you are, my little foal," said the lad.

"Yes," said the foal, "but if you'll send all the other foals to market and let me drink the milk of all the mares one more year, you'll see how big and sleek I'll be then."

Yes, the lad was ready to do that, so he sent all those twelve foals to market and went home again.

When he came back the next year to look after his foal and the mares, the foal was a yearling colt, so fat and sleek that the sun shone from his coat, and he had grown so big that the lad had hard work to mount him. As for the mares, each one had another foal.

"Well, it's plain I lost nothing by letting you drink all the milk of all my twelve mares," said the lad to the colt, "but now you're big enough to come along with me."

"No," said the colt, "I must stay here a year longer. Now send all the twelve foals to market and let me drink the milk of all the mares this year, too, and you'll see how big and sleek I'll be

71

by next summer."

Yes, the lad did that; and next year when he went up to the field, each mare had a new foal, and the dapple colt was so tall the lad couldn't reach up to his neck when he wanted to feel how fat he was; and so sleek he was, too, that his coat glistened in the sunshine.

"Big and beautiful you were last year, my Dapplegrim," said the lad, "but this year you're far grander. There's no such horse in the king's stable. Now you must come along with me."

"No," said the colt, "I must stay here one year more. Send the twelve foals to market that I may drink the milk of the mares the whole year, and then just come and look at me next summer."

Yes, the lad did that and went away home.

When he went back next year, the twelve mares had each a new foal, and as for Dapplegrim, the lad had never thought a horse could be so tall and stout and sturdy, for Dapplegrim had to lie down before the lad could mount him. It was hard work even then, and the horse's coat was so smooth and sleek, the sunbeams shone from it as from a looking glass.

This time Dapplegrim was willing enough to go with the lad, and when he came riding home to his brothers, they all clapped their hands, for they had never seen such a horse before.

"If you will get the best horseshoes and the grandest saddle and bridle you can find for my Dapplegrim," said the lad, "you may keep my twelve mares, and their twelve foals into the bargain."

Yes, his brothers were ready to do that. So the

lad got such strong shoes under his horse that the stones flew high aloft as he rode away across the hills, and he had a golden saddle and a golden bridle, which gleamed and glistened a long way off.

"Now for the king's palace," said Dapplegrim, "but be sure to ask the king to give me a good stable and good, clean fodder."

Yes, the lad said he would not forget, and it wasn't long, with such a horse under him, before he got to the king's palace.

The king was standing on the steps and stared and stared at the lad, now a man, who came riding along.

"Oho!" said he. "Such a man and such a horse I never yet saw in all my life."

And when the lad asked if he could get work in the king's household, the king was so glad he was ready to jump and dance as he stood on the steps.

"Ay," said the lad, "but my horse must have plenty of room in his stable and plenty of good, clean fodder."

Yes, Dapplegrim should have meadow hay and oats, as much as he could eat, and all the king's knights had to lead their horses out of the stable that Dapplegrim might have it all to himself.

So it wasn't long before the knights began to be jealous of the lad, and there was no end to the bad things they would have done to him, if they had only dared. At last they thought of telling the king the lad had said he was man enough to free the princess from the troll who had stolen her away long since. The king called the lad to him, and the lad kept on saying he never said he could do such a thing. But it was no good—the king wouldn't even listen. He said that if the lad did it he could have the princess and half the kingdom, but if he didn't, he should be killed. So the end of it was the lad was forced to say he'd go and try.

So he went into the stable heavyhearted, and Dapplegrim asked him at once why he was in the dumps.

Then the lad told him all, and how he couldn't tell which way to turn. "As for setting the princess free," he said, "that's stuff and nonsense."

"Oh, but it might be done, perhaps," said Dapplegrim. "I'll help you through; but first you must have me well shod. Ask for four kilos of iron and five kilos of steel for the shoes, and one smith to hammer and another to hold."

Yes, the lad did that and got both the iron and the steel and the smiths, and so Dapplegrim was shod both strong and well, and off went the lad from the courtyard in a cloud of dust.

But when he came to the troll's hill, he didn't know how to get up the steep wall of rock to the cave where the troll had hidden the princess. For you must know the hill stood straight up and down like a house wall and was smooth as a sheet of glass.

The first time the lad went at it he got a little way up; but then Dapplegrim's forelegs slipped, and down they went again, with a sound like thunder on the hill.

The second time he rode at it he got some way farther up; but then one foreleg slipped, and down they went with a crash like a landslide.

But the third time Dapplegrim said, "Now we must show our mettle," and went at it again till the stones flew heaven-high about them, and so they got to the top.

Then the lad rode right into the cave at full speed, caught up the princess, and threw her over his saddlebow, and out and down he rode before the troll had time even to get on his legs; and so the princess was freed.

The king was both happy and glad to get his daughter back. That you may well believe. "Thanks you shall have for freeing my princess," said he to the lad.

"She ought to be mine as well as yours, if you're a man who stands by his word," said the lad.

But somehow the others at the court made the king angry with the lad.

"Have her you shall," said the king, "but first of all, you must make the sun shine into my palace hall."

Now you must know there was a high, steep ridge of rock close outside the window, and it threw such a shade over the hall that never a sunbeam shone into it.

"That wasn't in our bargain," answered the lad, "but I see I must go and try my luck, for the princess I must and will have."

So down he went to Dapplegrim and told him what the king wanted, and Dapplegrim thought it might easily be done. But first of all, he must be new shod, and for that four kilos of iron and five kilos of steel were needed, and two smiths, one to hammer and the other to hold, and then they'd soon get the sun to shine into the palace hall.

So when the lad asked for all these things, he got them at once—the king was ashamed to say no. And what shoes Dapplegrim got! Then the lad jumped upon his back, and off they went, and for every leap that Dapplegrim gave, down sank the ridge fifteen metres into the earth, till there was nothing left of the ridge for the king to see.

When the lad got back to the palace he asked the king if the princess was his now, for no one could say that the sun didn't shine into the hall. But the others set the king against the lad again and he said the lad should have her of course, he had never thought of anything else, but first the bride must have as grand a horse to ride to church as the bridegroom had himself.

The king hadn't said a word about this before, and the lad thought he had now fairly earned the princess. But the king said if the lad couldn't do it, he should lose his life; that was what the king said.

So the lad went down to the stable in doleful dumps, and there he told Dapplegrim all about it; how the king had laid that task on him, to find the bride as good a horse as he had himself, else he would lose his life.

"And that's not so easy," he said, "for there isn't another horse like you in the wide world."

"Oh, yes there is," said Dapplegrim, "but it's not so easy to find him, for he lives in Hell. Still, we'll try. First I must have new horseshoes. Ask the king for four kilos of iron and five kilos of steel, and two smiths, one to hammer and one to hold, and twelve sacks of rye and twelve sacks of barley; and twelve loads of beef we must have with us, and twelve oxhides with twelve hundred spikes driven into each, and—let me see . . . a big tar barrel; that's all we want."

So the lad asked for all that Dapplegrim had said, and again the king was ashamed to say no, so the lad got all he wanted.

Well, he jumped up on Dapplegrim's back, and when he had ridden far far over hill and heath, Dapplegrim asked, "Do you hear anything?"

"Yes, I hear an awful hissing and rustling up in the air," said the lad. "I think I'm getting afraid."

"That's all the wild birds that fly through the wood. They are sent to stop us; but just cut a hole in the sacks, and then they'll be so busy eating the barley and rye, they'll forget us."

Yes, the lad did that. He cut holes in the sacks so that rye and barley spilled out. Then all the wild birds in the wood came flying around so thick that the sky was dark with them. But as soon as they saw the rye and barley they flew down and began to peck and scratch at it and then to fight among themselves. They forgot all about Dapplegrim and the lad and did them no harm.

So the lad rode on and on — far far over mountain and dale, over sandhills and moor. Then Dapplegrim pricked up his ears again and asked the lad if he heard anything.

"Yes, now I hear such an ugly roaring and howling in the wood all around, it makes me afraid."

Dapplegrim said, "That's all the wild beasts that roam through the woods, and they're sent out to stop us. But just throw down the twelve loads of beef. That will give them enough to do, and so they'll forget us."

Yes, the wild beasts in the wood, bears and wolves and lions, fierce beasts of all kinds came after them, but the lad threw down the loads of beef, and when the beasts saw the meat they began to fight for it among themselves and forgot all about Dapplegrim and the lad.

So they rode far away into many places the lad had never seen, and Dapplegrim didn't let the grass grow under him. At last he gave a great neigh.

"Do you hear anything?" he said.

"Yes, I hear something like a colt neighing loud, a long, long way off," answered the lad.

"That's a full-grown colt then," said Dapplegrim, "if we hear him neigh so loud such a long way off."

They travelled on still farther, and Dapplegrim gave another neigh.

"Now listen, and tell me if you hear anything," he said.

"Yes, now I hear a neigh like a full-grown horse," answered the lad.

"You'll hear him once again soon," said Dapplegrim, "and then you'll hear he's got a voice of his own."

So they travelled on and on and Dapplegrim neighed the third time. But before he could ask the lad if he heard anything, something gave such a neigh across the grassy hillside, the lad thought hill and rock would surely be split asunder.

"Now he's here," said Dapplegrim. "Make haste and throw over me the hides with the spikes in them, and throw down the tar barrel. Then climb up into that great fir tree yonder. When the horse comes, fire will flash out of both nostrils, and then the tar barrel will catch fire. Now, listen to me. If the flame rises, I win. If it falls, I lose. But if you see me winning, take off my bridle and throw it over the other horse's head, and then it will be tame enough."

So just as the lad had thrown the oxhides over Dapplegrim and cast down the tar barrel and climbed into the fir tree, up galloped a horse with fire flashing out of his nostrils, and the tar barrel caught fire at once. Then Dapplegrim and the strange horse began to fight. They bit and kicked with forefeet and hind feet till the stones flew heaven-high, and sometimes the lad could see them and sometimes he couldn't, but at last the flame began to rise, for wherever the strange horse bit or kicked, he met the spiked hides, and at last he had to yield. Then the lad got down from the trees and threw the bridle over its head, and then it was so tame you could have held it with a thread.

And what do you think? That horse was dappled, too, and so like Dapplegrim, you couldn't tell which was which. Then back to the palace rode the lad on the new dapple he had tamed, while the old Dapplegrim ran loose by his side. So when he got home, there stood the king out in the yard.

"Can you tell me now," said the lad, "which

is the horse I have caught and tamed, and which is the one I had before? If you can't, I think your daughter is fairly mine."

The king looked at both dapples, above and below, before and behind. "There isn't a hair's difference between them," he said, "and since you've got my daughter such a grand horse for the wedding, you shall have her with all my heart. But still we'll have one trial more to see if you're fated to have her. First she shall hide herself twice, and then you shall hide yourself twice. If you can find out her hiding place and she can't find yours, why then, you're fated to have her and so you shall have her."

"That's not in the bargain either," said the lad, "but we'll try, since you say so."

The princess went off to hide herself first. She turned herself into a duck, swimming on a pond that was near the palace. But the lad ran down to the stable and asked Dapplegrim what she had done with herself.

"Oh, just take your gun and go down to the edge of the pond and aim at the duck that is swimming about there. She'll soon show herself."

So the lad snatched up his gun and ran off to the pond. "I'll take a pop at this duck," he said, and took aim at it.

"No, no, dear friend, don't shoot. It's I," said the princess.

So he had found her once.

The second time the princess turned herself into a loaf of bread among four loaves on the cupboard shelf in the king's kitchen, and all looked so much alike that no one could say which was which.

But the lad went again down to the stable and told Dapplegrim that the princess had hidden herself and he didn't know at all what had become of her.

"Oh, just sharpen a good bread knife," said Dapplegrim, "and act as if you were going to cut a slice from the loaf next to the left-hand end of the row. You'll find her soon enough."

Yes, the lad was down in the kitchen in no time and began to sharpen the biggest bread knife he could lay his hands on. Then he caught hold of the loaf next to the left end of the row and raised his knife. "I'll just have a slice off this loaf," he said.

"No, dear friend," said the princess, "don't cut. It's I."

So he had found her twice.

Then it was his turn to hide, and he and Dapplegrim had settled it all well beforehand. First he turned himself into an insect and hid himself in Dapplegrim's left nostril. The princess went hunting him everywhere, high and low, and at last she wanted to go into Dapplegrim's stall. But he began to kick and bite so that she did not dare go near him, and so she couldn't find the lad.

"Well," she said, "I can't find you, so show me where you are," and in an instant the lad stood there on the stable floor.

The second time Dapplegrim told him to turn himself into a clod of earth and hide under Dapplegrim's hoof on the near forefoot. So the princess hunted up and down, out and in, everywhere. At last she came to the stable and wanted to go into Dapplegrim's stall. This time he let her come up to him, and she looked high and low, but under his hoofs she couldn't look, for he stood on his feet as firm as a rock, and so she couldn't find the lad.

"Well, you must just show yourself, for I'm sure I can't find you," said the princess, and as she spoke the lad stood by her side on the stable floor.

"Now you are mine indeed," said the lad, "for now you can see I'm fated to have you." The princess said it was so, and the king said, "Yes, it is fated to be, so it must be."

Then they got ready for the wedding and lost no time about it, and the lad got on Dapplegrim and the princess on Dapplegrim's twin, and then you may be sure they were not slow in getting to the church.

The Black Horse

ONCE THERE WAS a king, and he had three sons. And when the king died, the youngest son got nothing but an old, limping white nag.

"If this is all I get," said he, "I had best take it and go."

So he took the limping old horse and went straight along the road, sometimes walking, sometimes riding, until what should he see coming towards him out of the west but a young rider on a wild little black horse.

"I'm breaking my heart riding this wild horse," said the lad. "Will you give me your white horse for him?"

"No," said the king's son, "that would be a bad bargain for me."

"Never fear," said the rider. "You might make better use of him than I, for there is no place you can think of in the wheel of the world that the black horse will not take you."

So the king's son got the black horse and gave

away the limping white nag. Then he thought that he would like to be in the Kingdom Underwaves, where he had never been, for it was deep under the sea. And before sunrise on the morrow he was there.

Now King Underwaves was asking who of his people would go to seek the princess of the Greeks to be the bride of his son, Prince Underwaves. No one had offered to go, when who should come up but the king's son riding the black horse.

"You, rider of the black horse," said Prince Underwaves, "I put you under spells unless you have the daughter of the king of the Greeks here before the sunrises tomorrow."

The king's son went out to the black horse and leaned his elbow on the mane, and he heaved a sigh.

"Sigh of a king's son under spells!" said the horse. "Have no care. We shall do the thing that was set before you." So off they went.

And when they came to the great town of the Greeks, the king's son showed off his horsemanship. And the princess was looking out of the castle window, and the horsemanship pleased her.

Out she came and said, "Give me a ride on the horse."

"You shall have it," said he, "but the horse will let no man but me take the reins."

So she mounted the horse behind him and he was in the Kingdom Underwaves with her before sunrise.

"There you are, my hero," said the Prince Underwaves. "You, too, are the son of king, but

85

I am a son of success. Anyhow, we shall have no delay now, but a wedding."

"Just gently," said the princess. "Your wedding is not so near as you suppose. I will not marry till I get the silver cup that my grandmother and my mother had at their wedding. I need to have it at my own wedding."

"You, rider of the black horse," said the Prince Underwaves, "I set you under spells unless the silver cup is here before dawn tomorrow."

Out went the king's son and leaned his elbow on the horse's mane, and he heaved a sigh.

"Sigh of a king's son under spells!" said the horse. "Mount and you shall get the silver cup. The king of the Greeks is sitting in his castle with all his people gathered around him. When we reach the castle, you go in and sit in their midst. They will have the cup there, passing it from one to another. When the cup comes round to you, take it under your arm and come out with it, and we'll go."

Away they went and they got to Greece, and he went into the palace and did as the black horse bade. He took the cup and came out and mounted, and before sunrise he was in the Kingdom Underwaves.

"We had better get married now," said Prince Underwaves to the Greek princess.

"Slowly and softly," said she. "I will not marry till I get the silver ring that my grandmother and my mother wore when they were married."

"You, rider of the black horse," said Prince Underwaves, "let's have that ring here tomorrow at sunrise."

The king's son went to the black horse and put his elbow on his mane and told him how it was.

"This is the hardest task that ever was set before me," said the horse, "but there is no help for it. Mount me. There is a snow mountain and an ice mountain and a mountain of fire between us and the winning of that ring. It is right hard for us to pass them, but I can go where I must go."

Thus they went. Not far from the snow mountain it was bitter cold, but with a bound the horse was on top of the snow mountain. At the next bound he was on top of the ice mountain. At the third bound he went over the mountain of fire with king's son dragging at the reins to keep from falling.

Beyond the mountain of fire they came to a lake six kilometres long and six kilometres wide.

"Get down from my back," said the black horse, and the king's son dismounted, for he had never yet disobeyed the horse.

"Now I must go into the lake," said the horse, "and when I got out into it, the lake will take fire and blaze. If you see the fire going out before the sun rises, you will know I am coming. If not, go your way."

Out went the black horse into the lake, and disappeared, and the lake became flame. All night long was the king's son waiting beside the lake, and he wrung his hands and wept for his black horse. But at the hour when the sun was rising out of the water, the fire in the lake went out, and the black horse rose in the middle of the water with one single spike in the middle of his forehead and the ring upon its end.

He came on shore, and down he fell beside the lake.

Then down went the rider. He got the ring, and he dragged the horse down to the side of a hill, and fell to sheltering him with his arms about him. And as the sun was rising, the horse got better and better, till about midday, when he rose to his feet.

"Mount," said the horse, "and let us be gone."

The king's son mounted on the black horse, and away they went.

He reached the mountains, and he leaped the horse at the fire mountain and was on the top. From the mountain of fire he leaped to the mountain of ice, and from the mountain of ice to the mountain of snow. By morning he was in the Kingdom Underwaves.

"A king's son are you," said Prince Underwaves, "but a son of success am I. We shall have no more mistakes and delays but a wedding this time."

"Go easy," said the princess of the Greeks. "Your wedding is not as near as you think. Till you make me a castle, I won't marry you. Make me a castle beside which your father's castle will look like dishwater."

"You, rider of the black horse, make that," said Prince Underwaves, "before tomorrow's sun rises."

The king's son went out to the horse and leaned his elbow on his neck and sighed, thinking that this castle never could be made.

"There never was a turn in my road easier to pass than this," said the black horse.

And the king's son looked up and saw ever so many workmen and stonemasons at work, and the castle was ready before the sun rose.

"You are a son of success," said Prince Underwaves, "but I am a son of success, too. There will be no more mistakes and delays but a wedding now."

"No," said the princess. "Should we not first go to look at the castle? There's time enough to get married afterwards."

They went to look at the castle. "I see one fault," said Prince Underwaves. "We need a well inside so that water will be easy to fetch when there is a feast or a wedding in the castle."

"That won't be long undone," said the rider of the black horse.

The well was made, and it was seven fathoms deep and two or three fathoms wide, and they looked at the well on the way to the wedding.

"It is very well made," said the princess, "but for one little fault yonder."

"Where is that?" said Prince Underwaves.

"There," said she.

He bent down to look and she put her two hands at his back and cast him in.

"Stay there," said she. "If I am to be married, you are not the man but the hero who did each deed that has been done. And if he chooses, I will have him."

Away she went with the rider of the little black horse to the wedding. And the king's son was so happy with her that it was three years before he remembered the black horse or where he left him.

He got up and went out, and he was very sorry for his neglect of the black horse. He found him just where he had left him.

"Good luck to you, gentleman," said the horse. "It seems that you have now got something that you like better than me."

"I have not," said the king's son, "and I never will, but I forgot you."

"I don't mind," said the horse. "It will make no difference, if only you will obey me one more time. Raise your sword and smite off my head."

"I cannot do that," said he. "I cannot."

"Do it instantly," said the horse. "If not, I must do it to you."

So the king's son obeyed. He drew his sword and smote off the horse's head. Then he turned away and covered his face with his hands and wept with a doleful cry.

What should he hear behind him but "All hail, brother-in-law."

He looked behind him, and there was the finest man he ever set eyes upon.

"What made you weep for the black horse?" said the stranger.

"Because," said the king's son, "there never was a creature in this world that I was fonder of."

"Would you take me in his place?" said the stranger.

"If I could think you were the horse, I would, but if not, I would rather have the horse," said the rider.

"I am the black horse," said the young man.

90

"I was put under a spell, and many a man have I run to before you met me. None of them could manage me and they never kept me a couple of days. But when I fell in with you, you kept me till the time ran out and I could be free. Now you and your princess, my sister, shall go home with me to the castle of the king of the Greeks, and there we will make a celebration in my father's house."

And they lived happy and died happy
And never drank from a dry cappie.

The Raksh of Rustem

THIS IS THE STORY of Rustem, whom the Persians called "champion of the world," and it is the story of his horse, Raksh. For a thousand years before the birth of Rustem the shahs ruled Persia and made it into a great kindgom because they worshipped the god of light from whom all good things came. The gathered armies to fight against the demons of darkness and forced the demons to build for them a shining palace and a jewelled throne. From this throne the shahs gave commands to lesser kings who ruled only by the will of the shahs.

At last some of the shahs became puffed up with pride, forgetting the power of God. Then the light faded from the palace and the throne of Persia and the kingdom became weak, unable to subdue its powerful neighbours.

But it was written in the stars that a champion should come to protect Persia. During the rule of a good shah, a son was born to his chief

warrior. The father did not rejoice, for the child was strange, having snow-white hair, so he was called Zal, the old one, and was carried away to die exposed on the highest mountain of Persia, whose crest touched heaven.

Yet the child was destined to survive. At the top of the mountain lived a magical bird, a bird of wonder, who knew all things. Spying the deserted baby on the mountain slope, she foresaw that he would become the father of the champion of world, and she carried Zal in her talons to her nest and reared him with her own fledglings. And when he became a man, she carried him back to the world of men, giving him a feather from her wings. "I will never forsake you," she said. "If ever you need me, burn this feather, and I will come to help you."

Zal soon became a great warrior and served the shah well, but it was his fate to fall in love with a beautiful princess whose father was not friendly to the shah, and Zal and the princess Rudaba were forced to meet in secret. At last her father, hoping to win favour with the shah, gave in to his daughter's pleas and allowed a marriage. The shah, too, blessed the union because his wise men said "From Zal and Rudaba will come a hero who will make Persia the greatest kingdom on earth. He will bring peace to the hearts of the people, and in his time he will bring all wars to an end."

The birth of this hero was no easy thing. While Rudaba lay in childbed, she fell sick with a fever, and the doctor could do nothing for her. Zal despaired of her life. Then he remembered the feather given to him by the bird of wonder, and he threw it into the fire. At once the air was filled with the sound of rushing wings, and the bird appeared. She gave Rudaba a magic potion so that she was cured of her sickness and slept peacefully. While she slept, her son was born, perfect in form and beauty, and as big and strong as a year-old child. When Rudaba woke and saw him, she smiled and said, "His name shall be Rustem, which means 'delivered', because I am delivered from pain to joy."

Zal entered to the service of the shah, and Rustem remained for eight years in the country of his mother. At eight years of age, he asked for a horse and saddle, a helmet and a suit of armour, but Rudaba thought that it was only a child's whim. At ten, he killed a white elephant that had gone mad and was trampling all who came in its path, and Rudaba saw that the time had come to send him to his father to grow up as a man among men, learning the lessons of all Persian boys: to tell the truth, to shoot straight, and to ride.

It happened at this time that the shah died without heirs. This tempted an ambitious young prince of Turkestan to attack Persia and proclaim himself ruler. Then the people of Persia sent messengers to Zal, begging him to drive out the foreign invader. But Zal said, "I have never feared any enemy but old age, and now it has overcome me. I can only offer the help of my son Rustem, if he will give it. He is still a boy and should have a boy's pleasures, but he is as strong as a war elephant and can take his place with champions."

When Rustem heard his father's words, he

said, "Give me a horse and a weapon and I will ride against the invaders of my country."

Then Zal gave Rustem a great club that had belonged to his grandfather, and he told him to choose a horse from his own herds of fine Arab steeds, all graceful, swift, and intelligent. As each one was led before the boy, he pressed his hand on its back to test how well it could bear weight. And each of the horses shuddered and sank down on its haunches under the weight of his hand. Then Rustem saw a mare whose coat was the colour of gold, dappled with red. A colt ran beside her, his coat like hers and his chest and shoulders like a lion's. His mane and tail streamed back like golden flames. And Rustem threw a noose around the colt's neck and said, "This is the one I want, if he can bear my weight."

But the keeper, who did not know Rustem, said "Choose another. The mare will not let this colt be ridden. There are strange rumours about him. They say he is meant for only one rider, Zal's son Rustem. That is why the colt is called the Raksh of Rustem, the lightning of Rustem."

At this, Rustem laid hold of the colt's shining mane and swung himself up, saying, "I am Rustem". The mare ran at him fiercely, biting and striking out with her forefeet, but Rustem gave a great shout like a battle cry, "Rustem!" And when the mare heard it, she stood still and was calm. Then Rustem rode away on Raksh, as if on a streak of lightning. Now began the labours that Rustem accomplished for Persia, always with the help of Raksh, the matchless steed. He drove out the invaders from

Turkestan and again and again came to save his country.

While Rustem was still very young, it happened that a weak and foolish shah listened to a lying demon who came from Mazinderan and advised him to invade that enchanted country for its gold and jewels. Leading the army himself and asking no help from Zal or Rustem, the shah was met at the border by the huge army of Mazinderan. For two days a battle raged, while swords clashed, horses neighed, pawing the ground with their hoofs, and the dust rose to heaven under their trampling. Here the shah was defeated and led away as a captive with all the flower of his army. Demons covered them with darkness and they were blinded. Only one man escaped and carried a message to Zal, begging for his help.

But Zal was now of a great age, and he said, "I am too old to go. You, Rustem, saddle your good horse Raksh and ride to save Persia. Take the short road. It is the most dangerous one, but you can reach Mazinderan quickly."

Rustem set off at once. So swift was Raksh that he covered a two days' journey within twelve hours, and at nightfall Rustem lay down to rest in a thicket of reeds. Even a hero must sleep, but Raksh grazed and kept watch.

Now in the reeds a fierce lion was watching them, and he leaped upon Raksh. The great horse struck out at the lion's head with his hoofs and had trampled him to death when Rustem heard the noise of the fight. Seeing what Raksh had done, he reproached him, saying, "Foolish steed, who told you to fight with lions? If you had been killed, how could I have reached Mazinderan to rescue the shah?" Then he went back to sleep, but Raksh was sorrowful and downcast.

The next day they crossed the desert, burning hot and dry under the pitiless sun. Both horse and rider were perishing of thirst, and Rustem had commended his soul to God, preparing to die, when suddenly a ram appeared in their path, fat and healthy. And Rustem said, "No living thing could survive here except by a miracle. Let us follow this animal, since it must know where to find water." And behold, the ram led them to a spring of clear water by a cave. There Rustem and Raksh drank their fill, and Rustem bathed his tired horse. Then he lay down to sleep in the cave, saying to Raksh, "Do not take on a fight alone. If there is danger, wake me, and I will help you."

Later in the night a fiery dragon approached the cave. When Raksh saw it, he neighed and stamped with his hoofs to waken his master, but when Rustem opened his eyes, the dragon had disappeared by magic. Then Rustem was angry with Raksh, and said, "Do not waken me without reason, for I am very tired." Again he slept, and again came the dragon. Once more Raksh woke Rustem by stamping and neighing. But once again, when Rustem woke, there was nothing to be seen. When this happened a third time, Rustem hurled bitter words at Raksh and said, "If you wake me again without cause, I will kill you, even if I have to walk all the way to Mazinderan." And the heart of Raksh was heavy.

But Rustem was to learn how well he could trust the fidelity and intelligence of his horse. Once more the dragon approached the cave, while Raksh stood back, torn between his wish to avoid his master's wrath and his wish to save him. The dragon, thinking that the man was helpless without his horse, entered the cave. Then Raksh neighed and pawed the ground, and Rustem woke and saw the dragon. It fell upon him in fury and wound itself about him so that he could scarcely use his sword. But Raksh sprang upon the dragon from behind and tore its flesh with his sharp teeth until between them Rustem and Raksh destroyed the monster. Then Rustem praised Raksh and washed him again in the spring, and they went on together, glad at heart.

On their way, Raksh was hungry, so Rustem let him graze, seeing no owner from whom he could ask permission. He himself lay down to rest, but while he slept, a farmer came and saw Raksh in the pasture. Then the farmer beat Rustem with a stick and ran off to the ruler of that land, demanding vengeance for the damage that Raksh had done. And the ruler came against Rustem with an army. Rustem was angry in his turn, and, mounting Raksh, he cried, "Is this your courtesy to one man and a hungry horse? Now you will see that I am the thunderbolt and my horse the lightning, and we will scatter your army." And the whole army was routed by the valour of the champion with his club and sword, and by Raksh with his sharp teeth and mighty hoofs.

Then Rustem caught the ruler in the noose of

his rope, and said, "Shall I kill you, or will you lead me to Mazinderan where the shah of Persia is captive?"

The ruler wept and begged Rustem not to take that dangerous road, for he said it was guarded by lions and magicians and giants. Rustem said, "Lead me by that road and I will make you king of Mazinderan. Deceive me, and you die." Then the ruler agreed to show the way, and Rustem tied his rope to Raksh's saddle and sped off like the wind to Mazinderan with the man running beside him, whether he would or no.

Now when they came near Mazinderan, Raksh neighed so loud that the shah heard him, but his men could not believe that help had come until they heard the shout of Rustem that split the mountains as he attacked and killed the chief of the demons who held the city. The rest fled, and Rustem entered the tent where the shah sat, blind and helpless.

"I give thanks that you have come, my champion," said the shah, "but a great labour still lies ahead. When the white demond of the Seven Mountains learns of your victory over his legions here, he will come out of his lair with such a swarm of devils that even you cannot stand against them. Therefore, go to the mountains and take him by surprise. Slay him, and bring back the blood of his heart, for a wise man has told me that this will restore our sight. And may the tree of gladness grow green again for Persia."

Then Rustem forced his guide to go with him as before and rode away into the Seven

Mountains until he came to the gates of Hell, where a thousand evil spirits guarded the lair of the white demon.

The guide said, "Do not attack until noon. When the sun beats down most fiercely, even the demons must rest." And Rustem did as the man told him. When the sun was high, and all the devils slept, Rustem drew his sword. He shouted his battle cry, "Rustem!" and fell upon them like a thunderbolt, scattering their heads with his sword until all lay dead. Then he dismounted and entered the lair of the white demon with a roar that shook the mountain. From the depths of the cave the evil creature hurled an avalanche of stones and moved towards Rustem like a piece of the mountain itself. But Rustem met it in equal combat and struck blow for blow, tearing the monster to pieces, limb from limb. At last, he came from the cave holding the heart in his hands, and, wounded and weary, mounted Raksh. When they returned to Mazinderan, Rustem poured drops of blood from the heart of the white demon into the eyes of the shah and all his men, and again they beheld the light of day. Then the shah gave thanks to Rustem and, fulfilling Rustem's promise, made his guide king of Mazinderan. So peace came to the land.

Now it was written in the stars that Rustem should have a wife and a son and yet should have no joy of home and family. His marriage came about in this way. One morning in melancholy mood, Rustem saddled Raksh and rode off to hunt alone in the wild mountains to the north of Persia. When he had tired of sport, he lay down to sleep. Raksh was cropping the grass at a distance when a band of Tartar horsemen saw the beautiful dappled golden horse and, wishing to breed another of his kind, caught him with a noose. He fought desperately and killed two of the Tartars biting off the head of one and trampling another to death, but he could not escape the noose around his neck. The troop of horsemen surrounded him and led him, fighting all the way, to the palace of their king. There they hid him in the royal stable and told the king of the catch they had made. He was delighted and laid a plot to catch Rustem as well, for he knew that Rustem would soon come after his horse. This Rustem did, following the tracks of Raksh and the Tartar horsemen to the palace, where he angrily demanded the return of his steed. But the king met him with smooth words and promised that his men would try to find Raksh in the morning. Meanwhile, he said, Rustem must eat and drink and sleep. Then the king feasted Rustem with the best of food and wine and led him to a soft couch, telling him to sleep well.

In the night, Rustem was wakened by a veiled lady in perfumed robes, who came to him and said softly, "I am Tahmina, the king's daughter, and no man but my father has ever seen my face." Then she put back her veil and said, "Rustem, look at me. Is any prince of this earth worthy of me? No, only you are worthy, for I have heard of how you dared to go alone into Mazinderan and of how the earth trembles under your feet. I will be your wife if you will have me, and if we have a son, he will be like you in strength and valour. He could rule the world." Rustem saw that the princess was as lovely as the moon, but he hesitated. Then she said, "If you will be my husband, you shall have Raksh again by tomorrow morning, for I alone know where he is." Rustem answered, "I will take your hand in marriage," not knowing that the princess had said all these things at the command of her father. So Rustem and Tahmina were married with all due rites and ceremonies, but he could not linger in the pleasures of the palace; his duty was to Persia and the shah.

Before Rustem left his Tartar princess, he gave her an amulet, carved with the figure of the wonder bird who had so long ago saved the life of his father, Zal. "If we have a daughter, let her wear this in her hair," he said. "If we have a son, bind it on his arm." Then he returned to Persia and told no one that he had married a Tartar.

Rustem was never to see Tahmina again, but in time she bore their son, a boy so handsome and strong and with such a happy face that his mother called him Sohrab, the smiling one. To keep him safe with her she sent word to Rustem that he had a daughter, for she thought that if he knew he had a boy, he would take him from her into his own life of danger.

When Sohrab was a year old, he was a strong as a child of five. When he was five, he asked for a horse, and Tahmina gave him one of the breed sired in Tartary by Raksh. It was then that Sohrab demanded to know his father's name, and Tahmina told him the story of Zal and Rustem, and bound the amulet with the picture of the wonder bird on his arm. From this moment Sohrab had but one wish, to drive the shah of Persia from his jewelled throne and to make his father, Rustem, ruler over all the land, but this last he kept in his heart.

Rustem soon heard of the young leader in Tartary who had sworn to overthrow the shah, and with all the armed might of Persia he crossed Tartary, meeting no resistance until he came to the Oxus River. There Sohrab and a great army of Tartars came to face them. Sohrab strained his eyes to find the figure of a Persian warrior big enough to be his father, and begged his captain to point out Rustem. But some could not, and others would not, because they feared what might happen if Sohrab found his father and joined forces with him.

As the armies made ready to fight on the low-lying plain, the Persian captains urged Rustem to meet young Sohrab and destroy him in a single combat. But Rustem saw him from afar and said, "Alas, I have no son, and I would rejoice to have one such as this young man. It would grieve me to kill him, and he would surely fall at my hand. Let another man have the glory of the combat, if it must come." But the Persian chiefs answered, "Shall Sohrab boast that Rustem would not face him?" and at last they persuaded Rustem that he must fight Sohrab.

In the Tartar camp Sohrab watched only for Rustem, wishing not to fight him but to meet him in love and friendship. But the lying Tartar chiefs said, "Rustem is not here. He is far away. Fight against the greatest champion the

Persians can send. It will not be Rustem." They wished the combat to take place, for if Sohrab won, they thought they could control him, and if Rustem won, he would surely die of grief when he found that he had slain his son. In either case, the Tartar chiefs would easily overthrow the shah and rule Persia. So through lies and plots it was fated that father and son should meet each other in single combat.

As they stepped forward to do battle in sight of the two armies, each was strangely attracted to the other for a reason that neither could understand. Even as they made ready, Rustem said, "Young champion, the air is warm and soft, the earth is cold. If I fight you, I will kill you. Leave Tartary for Persia. We have need of heroes like you."

And Sohrab replied, "I cannot do what you ask, but tell me, are you not Rustem?"

"I am only the least of the shah's slaves. If you saw Rustem, you would not dare to challenge him," said Rustem. He thought to frighten Sohrab into giving up the fight against the strength of Persia. But Sohrab was angered by these words and would talk no more.

Then the two champions mounted their horses and fought with spears and with swords and with clubs until blood and sweat ran down their bodies, and neither could gain the victory. They parted only to rest and return to the fight, and Rustem thought that even his battle with the white demon had been nothing to this. Again they fought with arrows and with clubs, and Sohrab gave Rustem such a blow that he reeled beneath the stroke, but when night fell, neither could claim the victory, though both were wounded.

As Sohrab rested that night in the Tartar camp, he said to his captains, "My mind is filled with thoughts of this old man, and my heart goes out to him as if he were my father. Can it be so?"

But one of the chiefs answered with lying words, "I have often seen Rustem in battle. This man is not like him."

When the next day came, Sohrab and Rustem mounted their steeds and rode again against each other with a sound like thunder. From morning until sunset they fought. Then Sohrab seized Rustem about the waist and threw him to the ground and kneeled upon him and drew his sword. But Rustem said, "Are you too young to know the rules of combat? A worthy opponent is not killed at the first fall, but is given a second chance." This he said to save his life, and Sohrab believed him and let him go.

When they had rested, Sohrab returned to the fight like a giant, but Rustem rode towards him full of cares and fears, and he prayed to God to give him the victory. And God heard his prayer so that new strength came to him, and he shouted his battle cry, "Rustem!" When Sohrab heard that name he dropped his guard, and Rustem ran him through with his sword. Sohrab fell to the ground and he gave a great sigh in his pain and said to Rustem, "When my father Rustem knows that you have killed me, he will take his revenge."

Rustem sank down beside him and the earth became dark before his eyes and he said, "I am

Rustem, but you cannot be my son. I have no son." Yet his heart was full of foreboding.

Sohrab answered, "Open my armour and see the jewel on my arm. My father gave it to my mother as a token for me."

Rustem looked and saw the amulet with the sign of the bird of wonder. And tears flowed from his eyes and he cried aloud with sorrow, "I have been a man of war all my life. Have I now caused a noble son to perish?"

But Sohrab said, "Tears are no remedy. Weep not, for doubtless it was written that this should be so. Only let the armies go home, and let there be peace." With these words Sohrab died, and the beautiful horses, Raksh and his colt, came near at hand, and tears fell from their dark eyes.

Then Rustem took the body of Sohrab to Persia and built for him a tomb of gold, shaped like a horse's hoof as a sign that his son had been graceful and brave and strong.

Rustem would willingly have died because he had slain his son, but it was fated that he should live on and serve many shahs. Men say that for six hundred years his strong arm protected Persia. Yet the day came when he no longer served a shah but withdrew to the city where his father Zal and his mother Rudaba still lived. This he did because the shah who ruled at that time had agreed to pay tribute to the Roman emperor. And Rustem was ashamed that Persia was no longer free, and he refused to pay tribute. For this reason, and because the champion on the dappled golden horse was much honored by the people, he was a vexation to the king of his city. Therefore, the king sent for his son Sheghad, and said, "The old lion, Rustem, can still fight, but help me to be rid of him and of his steed, Raksh, and I will at once make you king in my place."

Sheghad was ambitious to be king, so he agreed. His father ordered a deep pit to be dug and lined with many sharp swords, lightly covered with branches and earth. Then Sheghad invited Rustem to a feast and a great hunt. And when they had feasted, Rustem took his bow and arrows and mounted Raksh. Sheghad ran beside him, leading him toward the pit. But Raksh, when he scented the newly turned earth, reared up and refused to go on. Rustem commanded him to go forward, but Raksh would not, because he was afraid for his master's sake. Then Rustem was angry, and he did what he had never done before. He struck Raksh with his whip. And Raksh was grieved in his soul and sprang forward and fell into the pit, and the sharp swords pierced his body and that of Rustem. And Sheghad looked into the pit with his face full of joy, and said, "Many have perished by your sword. Now you perish by the sword."

But Rustem said, "Death comes to all men. My time has come. Only grant me one favour. Give me my bow and an arrow. I would defend my body if a wild beast should come before I am dead."

Sheghad did as Rustem had asked, but suddenly, even as he saw that both Rustem and Raksh were near death, he was afraid and ran and hid himself behind a tree. Then Rustem with the last of his strength rose up in his saddle and set the arrow to his bow and shot straight, through the tree and through the heart of Sheghad. And as life left his body, Rustem gave thanks that he had avenged his own death.

When this news came to Zal and to Rudaba, their grief was boundless, and an army went to lay low all the house of the king who had betrayed their champion. Then they brought back the body of Rustem and of Raksh, his steed, and buried them together in a noble tomb carved out of everlasting rock, worthy of the greatest Persian heroes and of his truest friend, Raksh, who had served him to the end.

Notes on the Stories

THE EBONY HORSE

This story is taken from *The Arabian Nights*, popular literature in Arabic-speaking countries. The tales were collected about 1450 and reflect the Muslim customs and manners of life in Baghdad when Harun-al-Rashid rules as emperor in the time of Charlemagne. The stories travelled from China to Spain, probably along the trade routes. Antoine Galland translated many of the tales into French while Louis XIV was on the throne; retellings into English have often been based on his work. But Edward William Lane, who translated part of *The Arabian Nights* from Arabic to English between 1838 and 1840, gives a more sensitive impression of how the stories sounded to the people for whom they were told and written.

The masterpiece of the Latin poet Ovid (43 B.C.–18 A.D.) was his *Metamorphoses (Transformations)*, to which we owe our knowledge of many Greek myths. In simplest terms, the story of Phaeton is a "why story" telling why Mount Etna became a volcano, why the Libyan desert exists, why the Nile river still keeps its head hidden, and so on. Psychologically, the myth teaches that the youth who takes on the father's responsibility (of driving the horses) without preparation and initiation into adulthood is doomed to destruction. Apollo tries to prepare Phaeton by telling him the names of the horses, for in primitive theory a secret of control is to know and use the name of a person or thing. Phaeton in panic forgets the names. For today's readers, an interesting aspect of the story is in the horses themselves; the life-giving solar energy that comes from their fire also has the power to destroy life.

FINN'S MEN AND THE MEAN MARE

Standish Hayes O'Grady gives this story in his *Silva Gadelica*, 1892, providing an English translation that has been the source for my retelling as well as for several, by others, under different titles. The poem describing the Other World is part of "The Isles of the Happy," translated by the German scholar Kuno Meyer in *Selections from Ancient Irish Poetry*. Finn MacCool is thought to have lied about the third century A.D. and to have fought for the high king of Ireland, protecting the land from the raids of the Norsemen. But mythically we see him and his men, the Fianna, as fighters against darkness, since "Finn" means "the fair-haired" and may be another name for the sun god. Dermot was brought up by the Irish god of love and appears as both lovable and generous in the story.

THE HORSE WHO BUILT THE WALL

From the *Prose Edda* or *Younger Edda* of Snorri Sturluson (1178-1241) a rich heritage of Norse mythology has come down to us. The meaning of "edda" has been debated; it may come from "great-grandmother," from "earth," or from "poetry". All three meanings would be suitable for these ancient poetic tales of gods and giants in the days of Creation. The names of the horses, like many other names in Norse mythology, are difficult and have been omitted here. The giant's horse was Svadilfari. Dr. Hilda Davidson, authority on Norse myth at Cambridge University, says in a letter to me: "*Svadill* is a slippery place and *svadilfarar* means getting into a slippery place. This is a genuine horse name, perhaps for an animal which can keep up on the ice . . . or does it mean something like Calamity?" Odin's grey horse with eight legs was Sleipner, which may mean both "sly" and "slippery", perhaps combining the qualities of "slippery place" Svadilfari and sly Loki.

PECOS BILL'S WIDOW-MAKER

The United States is a young country, and the

white man's stories that grew from the folklore of the American continent are not old, as such stories go. Tales about Pecos Bill, the cowboy equivalent of the lumberman's Paul Bunyan, appeared in print for the first time as an article, "The Saga of Pecos Bill" by Edward O'Reilly, in the *Century Magazine* no longer ago than October 1923. After that came more articles, and chapters in some anthologies of American folklore. The most satisfying source for readers of any age who love the American West in James Cloyd Bowman's *Pecos Bill, the Greatest Cowboy of All Time*, 1937. Bill, along with Widow-Maker and Slue-foot Sue, was part of Walt Disney's cartoon movie, "Melody Time", 1948.

FALADA AND THE GOOSEGIRL

The folktale collection of the brothers Jakob and Wilhelm Grimm was first translated into English by Edgar Taylor and published between 1823 and 1826 as *German Popular Stories*. I include "The Goosegirl" as "Falada and the Goosegirl" because of the significant role played by the horse, who can speak, but speaks only to the true bride. Falada is helpless to prevent trouble, yet his gift of speech provides the clue to the crime of the false bride. More significantly, he offers the compassion of the animal friend when human help fails.

DAPPLEGRIM

The Norse tales collected by the great folklorists Peter Christen Asbjörnsen and Jörgen Moe were published in Norwegian in 1845. On the suggestion of Jakob Grimm, Sir George Webbe Dasent translated them into English as *Popular Tales from the Norse*, 1858. In "Dapplegrim" we recognize the incident that parallels the familiar "Princess on the Glass Hill" and catch the humorous style of Norse folk speech. We also hear echoes of other stories about mythical or folkloric horses. (See the note on "The Black Horse", below.)

THE BLACK HORSE

Joseph Jacob's long note on the story in *More Celtic Fairy Tales* compares this black horse with one in a myth from India and also points out its similarity to "the little hump-backed horse" of Russia and to the Norse "Dapplegrim". Myths travel as if on the wind that blows about the world; the Celtic black horse comes from a small island off the coast of Scotland, and indeed the ancient Celts thought of the west wind as a wild black horse. John Francis Campbell (1822–1885) collector of Highland folktales, heard the story of "The Black Horse" on the island of Menglay in 1862. He said of it that "the simplest explanation of this Menglay myth, fished out of the Atlantic, is to admit that 'the black horse' and all this mythical breed came west with men who rode from the land where horses were tamed, which is unknown."

THE RAKSH OF RUSTEM

The *Shah Namah*, "Epic of Kings", is the epic poem of Persia, now Iran. In this work, longer than the *Iliad* and *Odyssey* together, the poet

Firdusi (c. 940-1020 A.D.) recounted the glories of ancient Persia from Creation to the seventh century. During this legendary time the shahs ruled over an empire that included many smaller kingdoms and city states. They worshipped Ahura Mazda, god of light, also called Ormudz. Rustem is the Persian Hercules, many of whose exploits are omitted here in order to focus on Raksh, his horse, whose fidelity and intelligence make him a character as moving as any animal hero of literature.

Another Hippo Book to look out for:

Seal Secret

Aidan Chambers

0 590 70302 1   £1.50

William was furious when his parents didn't hire a caravan by the sea for the holiday as they normally did. Instead here they were in Wales, in "a dump in a wilderness miles from anywhere". To make matters worse they expected him to go camping with Gwyn, the neighbouring farm boy who didn't seem too keen on having him anyway. Gwyn didn't want him because he was secretly keeping a seal pup and when he told William his plan for it, he was aghast. Somehow he must rescue the baby seal, and without revealing Gwyn's secret because he had sworn an oath. Trying to rescue a large "sausage gone beserk" is not easy as William imagined and in the end he is greatful to Gwyn after all.